HEAD OVER BROKEN HEELS

Haley Brown

TABLE OF CONTENTS

Head Over Broken Heels

Head Over Broken Heels

For all the girls who live vicariously
through books and dream of a
story of their own...

FRIDAY

8 Days Until the Wedding

FRIDAY *playlist*

- long story short ———————— Taylor Swift
- People Watching ———————— Conan Gray
- Unwritten ————————— Natasha Bedingfield
- We Are Never Ever Getting Back Together
  (Taylor's Version) ———————— Taylor Swift
- Bad Love ———————————— Dehd
- Anything Could Happen ———— Ellie Goulding
- Mary's Song (Oh My My My) ——— Taylor Swift
- Don't Fade ———————————— Vance Joy
- Backyard Boy ——————— Claire Rosinkranz
- The Story of Us ——————— Taylor Swift
- Someone New ———————————— Hozier
- This Could Be Good ————— Morningsiders
- Something That I Want ——— Grace Potter
- Come With Me ———— Surfaces, Salem ilese
- Boyfriend ———————————— COIN
- Karma ———————————— Taylor Swift

Chapter 1

ONCE UPON A TIME....

It is yet another happily ever after.

Even though I can't relate, I'm always drawn to the romance section of a bookstore. My story thus far hasn't been quite as rom-com worthy as the ones set between the pages, but maybe that's why I'm so intrigued by them. The stack of paperbacks in my arms surely all end with *yet another happily ever after*.

I like to think that I can predict exactly what's going to happen by the end of most stories. Yet when it comes to my own life?… I clearly can't predict a thing. I can't even come *close*. If I would've known what to expect going into this very moment, I would've avoided this section of Wonderland Books. I would've avoided *him*.

Once I see Jesse, I quickly crouch to the floor and practically fall over due to the large stack of books that I'm holding. Unfortunately, he's my ex-boyfriend who ruined our three-year relationship by cheating on me. To make matters worse, it was Valentine's Day—of *all* possible days—when I caught him kissing Camille Fisher in the hallway. The breakup happened right then and there, which was my immediate, uncomfortable reaction after seeing how… *comfortable* they were with one another.

I open the book that's on top of my stack and use it to shield my face as I pretend to read. My light blonde hair swoops down over my eyes, and I leave it there to further hide myself.

Jesse should *not* be here. He's definitely not the bookstore type, and rarely would he agree to tag along on my trips here. I can't help but wonder how long it will be until he leaves—or how much time I have to escape. Thanks to my cowardly decision to cling to the floor, I can't see anything over the tall shelves.

I sigh, hastily making a decision. I set the books on the bottom shelf and make a mental note to come back for them later. If I check out now, he's sure to spot me. Slowly, I rise to a squat and peek around the edge of the bookshelf. I don't see him to my right or left, so I make a stealthy beeline for the exit.

"Finley?" A quiet voice questions from behind—one that I sadly and begrudgingly recognize.

I slowly turn to face him. "Jesse…." I say through gritted teeth.

He continues, the corners of his mouth upturning into a smile. "How have you been?"

Titling my head, I let out a huff. "What do you want?"

"I wanted to say that I'm sorry for—"

"I'm not having this conversation right now." I've avoided this conversation for the past four months, so there's no need for an explanation now.

"Finley, really," he continues, "I shouldn't have done what I—"

I swing my purse over my shoulder, pausing to look him straight in the eyes. "I'm over it. Just leave me alone."

He stays quiet for just a second, but Jesse's never been one to hold his tongue for very long. "I'm sorry, okay? I knew you'd be here since you weren't home. That's why I came to look for you."

"Oh, *great*," I say sarcastically. "First, you cheated on me, and now, you're stalking me."

"Just hear me out. I know you have the wedding in South Carolina this week. If your offer still stands as me being your guest, I would love to—"

"You have to be kidding," I bitterly laugh, trying to stay quiet and not draw the attention of others.

"If you give me another chance, I can make it up to you. I can—"

"No," I cut him off and let only a portion of my racing thoughts come spilling out. "Absolutely not. I gave you plenty of chances, and you blew them all. I'm not sure why you thought *stalking* me would change things, but it doesn't work like that. You are not going to be my plus one at the wedding...." My eyes never falter on their intense stare as I continue, "*because I already have one.*"

This is a big, fat lie. I do *not* have a plus one, nor has the thought crossed my mind—until now.

My cousin, Sierra, is getting married and invited the entire wedding party and their families to stay at the grand beach manor for a week in preparation for the big day. Jesse was supposed to be my plus one, but things have clearly changed, and he's the last person I'd want to spend the week with.

Although word travels fast in my extended family... no one knows that I've broken up with him. At the time, I was not ready to delve into the details, nor did I want anyone to feel sorry for me.

I'm still not too keen on explaining to Aunt Sheryl why she'll have to reconfigure her pristinely planned seating chart in his absence. Reexplaining the situation to everyone else doesn't sound like a walk in the park, either. Besides, this week is all about Sierra. I don't want the attention on me and my shattered love life. If only I could avoid the questions altogether.

I have roughly twenty-four hours before I leave town. Since the breakup, I've had months to mentally prepare myself. How could I have forgotten that he was my plus one? Better yet, how was a lie about my so-called date the first thought that came to my mind?

Without another word, other than my racing thoughts, I walked straight out the glass doors and left Jesse standing speechless in Wonderland Books.

If only I was better prepared, I could've found someone else to tag along weeks ago. Now that I'm hyper-focused and my adrenaline is still pumping, I happen to notice every male I pass on my way home. I come to the realization that there truly are no possible suitors in my small town of Whitefield, Georgia.

On top of wanting to spare myself the questions from my extended family, I want to prove to Jesse that I don't need him any longer. I want to show him that I've moved on, which is why I keep an open mind as I pass familiar faces… even if they wouldn't normally make the cut.

Example #1: Otto Jones. Here he is now, rolling out of the video game store—literally *rolling* with his Heely's and a bowtie. He's the notorious weird kid in school, often showing up in a full tuxedo and a fedora. He is single, yet totally out of the question.

I slow to a stop at the red light near Mountain Mart as a white Jeep pulls up beside me. *Example #2: Brody Holland.* He's taken by the cute brunette sitting beside him. For the past year, they've been in a very committed relationship, and for that reason, Brody is an obvious no, as well.

As I turn into my neighborhood and leave the slightly more civilized side of town behind me, I spot someone walking his dog. *Example #3: Mr. Monroe.* Ew. With him, there are two deciding factors that make him the *worst* possible suitor thus far. One: he's a solid thirty-five years older than me, and two: he was my history teacher from freshman to senior year. I do my best to not shudder… and I fail tremendously.

Clearly, finding a plus-one in less than twenty-four hours is much easier said than done. Even if I could, there's no way my parents would agree to some random dude hijacking our family vacation. What am I *thinking?*

Once parked in my driveway, I shut off the car's ignition and hop out, keys rattling. Date or no date, I have things to do—such as packing.

"Hey, Fin!" A voice calls out, smiling as he waves from his front yard.

I turn to face the dark-haired, brown-eyed… *Example #4: Cole Baxter.* He's my lifelong friend and next-door neighbor, yet we're polar opposites.

Where I like to listen to music from this decade, Cole prefers to live vicariously in the past. He's competitive, whereas I'm just there for the participation award.

Our moms have been best friends since they were little girls. Once they each married the man of their dreams, they decided to fulfill all their *Keeping Up With the Jones'* aspirations by buying homes right next to one another. Cole and I are only fifteen days apart. He's older, and he won't let me forget it…. *Ever.* Neither will our moms. We have repeatedly been told the story of how Mrs. Clara surprised my mom with her ultrasound picture, only for my mom to do the same just a few seconds later—talk about perfect timing.

Growing up, our families created a routine that has stuck like glue. Every Sunday is breakfast at the Brooks'—my house. Wednesday is Game Night, typically hosted by the Baxters. It almost always ends with someone—namely, Cole and myself—fighting over who gets to deal the cards. Friday is a joint family dinner, which I'll be attending at their house in just a few hours. The weekend is a free-for-all. Our front doors stay open as family members cross paths, driveways, and flower beds more than multiple times a day.

Cole and I meet up near our invisible property line. This happens to be perfectly aligned with the treehouse our dads built us over a decade ago.

"What are you up to?" I ask as my rattling keys finally come to a stop.

"Nothing much." He shrugs. "I just got back from picking up Cassie from her ballet class. What about you?"

"I unfortunately just got back from a run-in with Jesse." I explain the key points of my conversation with him.

"I can't stand that guy," he says once I finish.

"Ditto," I sigh. "Well, I need to start packing for this week, but I'll see you at dinner tonight."

"See you later," he responds.

I shovel through my dresser drawers as I attempt to piece together outfits. All the while, my thoughts are still racing, causing me to fixate on issues—and a person—I've tried to forget.

Once I was past the initial shock of having my heart broken, I realized that I wasn't *actually* *brokenhearted* over Jesse. That's at least what I keep telling myself, anyway. More than anything, I felt—and still feel—betrayed.

In my mind, maybe I wasn't head over heels because we didn't live a fairytale life complete with grand gestures and romantic dates.

Once upon a time, I liked Jesse. I even loved him, possibly more than I loved myself. On a daily basis, he expressed his love for me, and I believed it... until he cheated. Because he's the only love I've ever known, it made me rethink everything. For my own selfish reasons, it makes me reluctant to love again... *because what if?*

What if... no relationship measures up to the ones that authors spend months planning? From the first chapter to the plot twist and beyond, it's usually created with a happy ending in mind.

What if... I put together all twenty-six letters in a story of my own, and the words don't create what I've envisioned in my daydreams?

What if... I can't fall for anyone else? I practically know everyone in this small town, and I certainly can't picture any of the Whitefield boys being my Prince Charming.

As I struggle to pull my suitcase down from the top shelf of my closet, I ponder over the boys whom I passed today. *Otto Jones*: out of the question. *Brody Holland*: taken. *Mr. Monroe*: a terrifying thought. *Cole Baxter*: strictly a friend.

I practically drop the suitcase onto the floor, nearly falling over it. It's not even packed yet, and it already weighs too much. As I let out a huff, I glance out my bedroom window. Now playing soccer with his little brother, I spot him once again—*Cole Baxter*. I see him every day. The sight of him is nothing new, yet the thought that pops into my head is completely foreign to me.

There's never been the slightest inkling of romantic feelings between us... but maybe there doesn't need to be.

Maybe... we can fake it.

Chapter 2

FAKE IT TILL YOU MAKE IT

I shake my head. *"Absolutely not,"* I tell myself. The thought of fake dating Cole is so ridiculous, it would never work. But then again… maybe this far-fetched, absurd idea is the exact solution that I'm looking for.

I spend most of the next half-hour reeling over whether or not I should ask Cole to come with me. I still think it's a little bit ludicrous, but I'm also thinking that it could work.

With nothing to lose other than my feigning dignity, I decide that it's worth a shot. I walk outside, interrupt his game of soccer, and motion to the treehouse that sits on the base of our backyards.

"Everything okay?" he questions warily. "You whisked me away just in time. I was about to lose."

I begin talking before I can second-guess myself on whether or not this is a good idea. "You remember what I said earlier about Jesse, right?"

Cole nods. "Yeah, why? Did he do something else?"

"*No...*" I draw out the word. "It's more like *I* did something else. When I told you that story, I may or may not have left out one *minor* detail."

"And what's that?"

"Once he tried to invite himself back on the trip, I told him that he wasn't going because I already had a plus one. That was clearly a lie, and I had no intention of *actually* finding a date... but then I started thinking."

"About...?" he presses.

"If I hypothetically *could* find someone, it would prove to Jesse that I'm over him. The bad news is, I leave tomorrow and my options are pretty limited." I tell him about the very few guys I've seen in the past two hours.

"I hate to break it to you, Fin, but you can cross me off that list."

"That's what I was thinking, however..." I begin to smile.

He must realize what I'm implying because he starts shaking his head and protesting before I can get the words out. "Nope, not happening. I love you, but definitely not in the way where I'm going to *date* you."

"That's the thing—we don't have to *actually* date. Obviously, it wouldn't be real. It could be like the last book I read—we can fake date."

Cole bursts into laughter.

"I'm serious!" I proclaim. "You can come with us to South Carolina for the wedding, and you'll practically get a free vacation out of it. All you have to do is put up with my family for a week, pose for a few pictures, and —at best—hold my hand a time or two. Then, we can stage a breakup."

"This does not sound like a good idea."

"Think about it, Cole. We have nothing to lose. For one, our families already act like we're destined to be together. Two, it'll further prove to Jesse that I could not be more over him than I already am. And three, it could possibly save me from answering humiliating questions about my ex cheating on me. I'm really not mentally prepared to talk about that."

Cole crosses his arms over his chest, thinking it through. "So, I'm the Prince Charming who could save you from five minutes of an awkward conversation?" *5 minutes?* He obviously doesn't remember my grandmother.

"Yes, pretty much. We just fake it till we make it through the week. Then it can be over."

"What's in it for me?" he presses.

"For real? Did you not just hear me mention the week-long vacation in the grand beach manor? All of that and more, just for the small price of pretending like you enjoy my company."

"I do enjoy your company!" he protests.

"So…" I pause, grinning. "What could go wrong?"

"Umm, a *lot*?"

"Okay, forget that question, then. Think about what could go *right*. You could save this little ole' damsel in distress from public humiliation. I could be like Rapunzel, trapped away in a tower as Mother Gothel —AKA my aunts—tries to interrogate me into explaining my love life. And I'd be left without anyone there to save me! Unless… one certain someone found his way to the tower. Or in this case, you could rescue me ahead of time."

He chuckles, uncrossing his arms. "Fine, I get it! I'm in, Drama Queen."

"Thank you, thank you!" I jump up excitedly.

"Under one condition," Cole hesitates. I raise my eyebrows, eager for him to continue. "Tonight, I get to tell our families that we're dating. You said it yourself, they already act like we should be in love with each other. Our moms have waited over eighteen years for this. *I'm about to sell the crap out of this fake relationship.*"

Oh goodness… what have I gotten myself into?

SATURDAY

7 Days Until the Wedding

SATURDAY playlist

- Saturday Sun ———————————— Vance Joy
- Come To The Beach — Winnetka Bowling League
- Vacation ———————————— The Go-Go's
- Almost (Sweet Music) ———————— Hozier
- Sit Next to Me ———————— Foster The People
- Dirty Little Secret ——— The All-American Rejects
- Dover Beach ———————————— Baby Queen
- Mastermind ———————————— Taylor Swift
- Cool Kids ———————————— Echosmith
- Destination ———————————— Nickel Creek
- Fun ———————————————— Sun Room
- Heartbreak Yellow ———————— Andy Davis
- Supermassive Black Hole ——————— Muse
- Just Friends ———————————— Jonas Brothers
- Call It What You Want ——————— Taylor Swift
- Perfect Places ———————————— Lorde

Chapter 3

THE RULES

When we were nine, Cole and I made a pact that we believed could one day alter the course of our adult lives. I'm not sure what kind of pacts other nine-year-olds make, but I don't think a marriage pact is the most popular topic on the playground.

That's right—*a marriage pact.*

Between our conversations of annoying classmates and our favorite Disney movies, we agreed to marry one another when we turn thirty. This came with rules, of course. All good pacts do.

Rule #1: If either of us were already married, the deal was off. *Obviously.*

Rule #2: Well… maybe we only had one rule. We *were* children, after all. Even so, we shook on it in the treehouse—that practically made it a legal law.

Albeit we haven't spent any time shaking hands in our old treehouse, today we'll begin our journey on a newfound pact.

It's an hour-and-a-half drive from our hometown to Sunrise Beach, South Carolina. My parents' car is filled with my three younger siblings and all their belongings, so Cole and I drive alone in his minivan, which is technically his mom's.

"I have a question," he pipes up from behind the wheel.

Wordlessly waiting for elaboration, I turn to him, afraid of what he may ask.

"Before we get in over our heads with this whole fake dating thing, how exactly is it going to end— dramatic fighting or a mutual agreement? I can cause a scene if you need me to."

"Oh, geez," I pause for a moment, thinking it through. "I think it should end mutually for sure. As much as I would personally *love* to see the dramatics play out, that's not the best call for our families' sake."

Cole nods. "I think both of our moms would be in complete hysterics if we crushed their dreams like *that*."

I chuckle, agreeing with him. "Oh, one hundred percent. I think they're still holding out hope for our old marriage pact. We can call things off at the end of next weekend. That seems like enough time to make it believable for the wedding, to say that we tried to make it work…."

"…And enough time to prove that it didn't," he finishes.

"Exactly." I make a motion with my hands as I speak as if it's obvious. In my mind, it is. "We'll go back to our old ways with ease—the friends and neighbors who were always destined to be more."

Cole chuckles. "As our moms would say."

I glance out the passenger window as the '*Come Again Soon!*' sign passes in a blur. In a little over one week, we'll be welcomed back into the quaint lake town with open arms. For now, we're leaving familiar waters as we travel Northeast, heading into a week of uncertainty, extended family shenanigans, wedding-related events, and hopefully… *fun*.

I turn to face Cole. "I feel like if we're going to do *this* correctly, we need to set some boundaries—rules, so to speak."

"If our inevitable breakup is Rule #1, what's Rule #2?"

We discussed this briefly yesterday, but I confirm, "We'll occasionally need to hold hands."

"That's easy enough."

"Good," I say bluntly.

He lifts a finger. "As long as you don't have freakishly weird, sweaty hands that I've never noticed."

"*Seriously?*" I chuckle while raising my hands in the air. "No need to worry."

Cole continues. "I do have my own request for a rule, though."

Grabbing my water bottle from the cupholder, I manage a "*Hmm*?" as I take a sip.

"We don't kiss."

I nearly choke on my drink. This took a slight turn from naive handholding for the sake of appearances.

"*Definitely* agree on that one!" I call out, finally finding my words. "That does not need to happen this week... *or ever.*"

"Agreed."

I try to think of another rule, *anything* other than the discussion at hand... and not a single thing comes to mind. Cole turns up the radio and fills the silence with awkward commercials of car dealerships. We must be out of our typical radio range because this seems to be the only entertainment this station has to offer. One after another, each dealership claims to have *the best* deals, *the best* leather seats, and *the best* interest rates. The only thing that isn't mentioned in the ads is *the best* conversation starter, which I'm desperately searching for.

I keep the cringeworthy momentum in full swing. "We need to seem like a real couple. We should go on a *real* date."

He quickly turns to me before looking back at the road. "*Excuse me?*"

"Sorry—a real, *fake* date! I'm sure we'll be doing most things with my family, but we should probably do some solo stuff too."

"Okay, we'll make it believable," he says. "Strictly business."

"It doesn't have to be much, but we do need to sell it," I finalize.

"*Selling* is what I do best." Cole smiles proudly.

I think he's heard too many ads considering his marketing tactics. You would guess he's majoring in marketing and business. Although come to think of it, I'm not too sure what he's majoring in at all. A pang of guilt hits me with this realization. Over the past few years, I've been so involved with Jesse. Not to mention, the past few months have been filled with Jesse *drama* as well as finals and graduation. I've hardly had time to talk to Cole. When I have, it didn't feel like the same level of closeness that we've shared in the past.

"One more addition," he adds. "Tell no one."

"Well, *duh*. I thought that one was pretty self-explanatory."

He lifts his hands up in surrender. "Hey, I still had to throw it in there. Your picks have been pretty self-explanatory as well."

I scoff. "I'll try to pretend that I didn't take any offense to that."

Cole places a hand on my shoulder with a sly smile. "We're not really dating. Take all the offense you want, *Sweetheart*."

I roll my eyes and do my best to hide the smile forming on my lips. As much as he tries to act all serious and broody, I know that he doesn't have a mean bone in his body. He once pushed over his school bully in first grade, only to apologize profusely.

Now reaching into the glovebox, I shovel through a mountain of old receipts, an owner's manual, and enough plastic silverware to feed an entire village.

"What are you looking for?"

"Something to write on." I grab a random receipt and examine it. The once-black words have faded to a light grey, and the date is fully illegible. I hold it up to him. "Is a receipt from Josephine's Pizza okay for me to use?"

He shrugs. "Works for me. My mom will never notice that it's gone."

"Great." I find a pen amidst my glovebox scavenger hunt and press the tip down with a satisfying *click*. Pulling my feet into the seat and placing the paper on my thigh, I begin writing. "Self-explanatory or not, it's best that I write the rules down—just in case." I shoot him a glare.

"What's with the look?" he protests. "You act like I'm going to be breaking all your rules."

"You never *knowww*," I say in a sing-song tone. "My irresistible bedhead and pimple patches are a force to be reckoned with. You may fall in love with me after all."

He barks out a rough laugh. "And what if I do?"

I smile, lifting the wrinkled receipt with my loopy handwriting. "Then we have proof that you don't follow rules."

"Touché," he says. "Why don't you just type everything on your phone? That seems like it would be much faster."

"1: We have a long stretch of road ahead of us, so I have *plenty* of time to write down five rules. 2: My phone is a piece of junk with no storage space, a shattered screen, and a death wish."

"And you won't buy a new one... *why* exactly?"

"Because this ten-year-old receipt works just fine at the moment."

"Translation," he interjects, "you're a soon-to-be broke college student trying to save money?"

"Yep, pretty much." I sigh. "I've been putting off getting a new phone until *this* one kicks the bucket."

Cole taps the GPS on his—*perfectly working*—phone, causing the screen to light up. He looks at the dashboard, then turns to me. "Well, you may want to use your death wish of a cellular device to let your mom that we're going to be a few minutes behind schedule. We need to get gas before we're stranded."

STOPPING TO REFUEL. WE'LL BE THERE SHORTLY.

— Rule #1: The inevitable breakup.

— Rule #2: Occasionally hold hands.

— Rule #3: No kissing.

— Rule #4: a real "Fake" date.

— Rule #5: Tell no one!

♡ Finley

Cole

Chapter 4

HOLLOW OAK

"You have reached your destination," the GPS echoes, robotic and monotone. I practically bounce in my seat with excitement and rising anticipation as we pull onto the property of the *Hollow Oak Beach House.*

It's on the outskirts of Sunrise Beach, just barely within the limits of the small town. Hollow Oak is the stunning venue and manor where the wedding is being held.

We pass through the golden gates and drive up the long, concrete driveway that leads to the house. The two-story house gleams a bright white against the blue sky. The landscaping that surrounds the house is impeccable. From the shrubs trimmed to perfection, the colorful flowers that line the property, and the oak trees that stand tall above the house, it's all *stunning.*

"Whoa, this place is huge," Cole remarks as he pulls the keys from the ignition.

"You're telling me," I breathe out.

Looking to my left, I notice my family's car. It's a little shocking to see that they arrived before us, considering how many bathroom breaks my younger siblings typically need.

"You ready to do this thing?" I ask, unbuckling my seatbelt.

Cole does the same, looking hesitant to get out. "Let's do it."

As I open my door and hop out, the front door swings wide open. Her brown hair is styled freely in her signature long bob. She's running up to the car before I can make it to her. "McCall!" I squeal.

She grins, pulling me in for a hug. In true McCall fashion, it's tighter than necessary and speaks more than a thousand words.

McCall and I are cousins; our moms are sisters. If Mrs. Clara is my mom's closest friend, Aunt Kira—McCall's mom—is her second. We live over three hours apart, and yet they still talk every single day. Their phone calls span from work lunch breaks to any free time they can find at home. Most days, if I'm having a conversation with my mom, Aunt Kira is more than likely on the other end of the line, listening in as well.

Despite the distance between us, our families meet up a few times throughout the year. Due to the craziness of my senior year—and McCall's—this is the first time we've seen each other since Christmas. McCall and I talk pretty regularly by text or FaceTime, yet we're nowhere near surpassing the sheer amount of phone calls our moms partake in on a daily basis.

The hug loosens, but our smiles don't fade.

"How's everything?" she asks. "I've missed our weekly recaps lately!"

I nod a tight-lipped smile, holding in countless stories that I've been saving for this week with her. "Pretty good, super busy! You know how's it been with... graduation and everything."

I may have *purposefully* left out a very key detail in my quick recap: *Jesse and I broke up. It's awful, I know! I even have my mom sworn to secrecy.*

Naturally, my mom would tell Aunt Kira, who would then gossip to Aunt Sheryl—my mom's oldest sister. To tell my Aunt Sheryl *anything* in reality... means telling *everyone everything.* She may even share made-up details to quote-unquote, *'spice up the drama'.*

Despite the guilt gnawing away at me over keeping McCall from such a huge part of my life, I continue. "How have you been? December to June is *far* too long of a gap without seeing my favorite cousin."

"I heard that, Finley!" A new voice sounds. I turn, seeing Sierra walk down the front steps to meet us. She's wearing a white tank top with flowy shorts that perfectly match the blonde of her hair.

"If it isn't the bride herself!" I beam. "You're also my favorite."

Although two of my cousins have rapidly appeared, another comes behind them, scoffing. Malik—

he's McCall's older brother, and he has the same dark hair and high cheekbones to prove it. Other than Cole, he was my biggest tormenter growing up. Still, despite his incessant desire to work out and constantly pick on me, I love him to death.

I love them *all* to death.

We're all standing in a circle as one more person joins us. He squeezes in beside me as he says, "Hey, guys."

I'm not sure why the sight of Cole standing next to us surprises me. Maybe it's the sight of my worlds colliding, like when you throw a birthday party and invite both your school friends *and* your sports friends. It's the fine line between being excited that they're all together... and also praying that everyone gets along.

In Aunt Sheryl's words, I think I may have *'spiced up the drama'* all on my own by bringing him here.

Luckily, most of my family has met Cole before. He was always present during the holidays we hosted at my house, but it's been quite a few years since then.

I'm the first to speak up. "Oh! I almost forgot to reintroduce all of you. This is Cole," I pause for a moment, mentally preparing myself to say the words aloud for the first time, *"my boyfriend."*

"No way!" McCall exclaims. "Cole, like *the* Cole who lives next door to you?"

Sierra and Malik's mouths drop open as they have the same realization of familiarity.

"That's me," Cole chuckles.

McCall turns back to me, clearly not losing the expression of pure *shock* spread across her face. "Finley, how have you not told me this yet?"

"It all happened pretty fast," I respond.

Cole doesn't do a great job of stifling his laughter. "Oh, you have *no* idea!"

I resist the urge to elbow him. Truly, I only stop myself because it doesn't seem like a very *'in-love'* thing for me to do.

"I still remember our games of tag in your front yard. I think we need a redo now that I've outgrown my scrawny, uncoordinated phase," Malik boasts.

Cole gives him a firm pat on the back. "Just tell me the time and place, man. I'm in."

Sierra's watch lights up, momentarily grabbing her attention. She begins, "Well, I hate to break up the reunion, but the two of you got here just in time. My parents are about to start their meeting, and the entirety of the Hollow Oak Beach House has been—and I quote—*requested.*"

"Oh, geez!" McCall places her palm on her forehead.

Cole leans in close to me and whispers, "Meeting?"

I shrug and follow Sierra's lead. This is sure to be interesting. Anything involving her parents often is. Very, *very* interesting.

Head Over Broken Heels

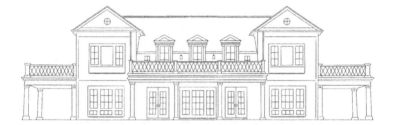

Chapter 5

BABE

Sierra's mom is my Aunt Sheryl. Yep, the same Aunt Sheryl who would have freaked out if I had screwed up her seating charts. She's also the one who's known to fuel herself with more coffee than oxygen.

Sierra's dad is Eddie. He's my uncle, but I don't dare to call him that. According to him, being called *Uncle Eddie* makes him feel old. He's pushing sixty, yet he likes to hang out with—in his words—*the cool kids*. Known for his crazy game ideas, he always goes out of his way to plan something fun for the family to do. Granted, he typically ends up taking charge, threatens to bench his teammates, and swears he's going to whip us into shape.

Despite being an only child who was raised by two of the most entertaining people I know, Sierra has turned out just fine. She received the best qualities of both parents, while she avoided their more questionable traits. However, I will admit that her parents' behaviors have led to *many* interesting events over the years.

Thanksgiving 2011: Aunt Sheryl assigned each family a certain dish, and the menu was to be followed to perfection. Thinking that *anything* would be *perfect* at our large family gathering was her first mistake. My mom made the unintentional mistake of bringing deviled eggs—which were previously assigned to Aunt Kira. We then had double the eggs and a negative amount of homemade gravy. I understand that gravy is an important dish, but you can *never* have too many deviled eggs. Based on the uproar of Aunt Sheryl's theatrics, you would've thought the turkey had come back to life, escaped from the oven by itself, and strutted out the front door. If I was the turkey, *I totally would have.*

We waited a few, purposeful years before allowing the Cooper household to host a holiday again.

Christmas 2016: Eddie's competitive spirit was ready to shine after opening gifts. He commenced an indoor 'snowball fight' with balled-up wrapping paper. We were all having a great time until he got a little too carried away. With one hard throw, he knocked a picture frame off the wall and onto my grandmother—an innocent bystander to his madness. Grandma Rose laughed it off but frequently reminds him that he almost spent his Christmas in the ER with her. She still jokes about the time he was nearly *'framed'* for her murder.

I have no clue what they have planned for us now, but I feel as if I should be slightly worried.

Walking into Hollow Oak, the interior matches the elegant, yet cozy aesthetic set on the exterior. People fill the area, sitting on the grey couches and occupying the dining room bar. They all face Aunt Sheryl and her oversized whiteboard in the center of the room. There are no extra seats, so Cole and I settle for a spot on the floor. McCall plops down to my right, pulling her feet in until she's sitting crisscrossed.

"Alrighty, folks!" Aunt Sheryl claps her hands and halts the chatter that is spreading around the room. "Family and friends, y'all listen up."

Cole tenses, and I have the weird feeling that I'm amidst a parent-teacher conference.

My aunt continues. "We're all here because Sierra requested to spend the week before her big day with all of you."

"Love you guys!" Sierra calls out to the room. A chorus of *love you too* is spread around the open area.

"This house," Aunt Sheryl continues on as if nothing was said, "is my responsibility this week. Food will be provided at large family events throughout the week. I will hand out our itinerary here shortly."

Heads nod as everyone is listening intently.

"You may be wondering about your daily meals," Aunt Sheryl points out. "Feel free to turn into hunters and gatherers."

Cole slowly turns to me, his eyes displaying a fearful expression. "*What?*" he mouths.

I shrug, feeling just as clueless and slightly afraid.

"Just kidding," she remarks with a sly grin. "Although the looks on your faces were priceless! We have stocked most of the basic ingredients in the fridge and pantry, which you are all welcome to use. However, most of you will be assigned one meal to cook for the manor."

Eddie chimes in now. "Our lucky chefs will not be marked on the itinerary. This surprise will be completely left up to chance."

Cole raises his hand like this truly *is* a parent-teacher conference. Mortified, I try to pull his arm down before he brings attention to us. It stays in the air as he jokes, "Do frozen pizzas count as a meal?"

"*Absolutely not.* Nice try…" Aunt Sheryl pauses for a moment, trying to place his name with a puzzled look. "*Young man,*" is what she decides on.

Behind us, Eddie rises from the couch. "Alright, enough of the details. It's time to get the ball rolling."

Uh oh, here we go.

"As you may or may not have noticed, this is the house of the bride. The only people staying here are Sierra's family, friends, bridal party—" he glances at Cole before continuing—"and guests. The white abode next door is for the groom and his entourage."

Truthfully, I didn't even notice the other house. I must have missed it in the miniature family reunion that abruptly ended with us scurrying inside.

Eddie holds his open palms in front of him as he goes on. "Now, before our families join together as one, *we are going to beat the crap out of each other.*" His hands clap together with a loud, echoing *bang.*

McCall jumps beside me, startled by the noise.

My Grandma Rose speaks up. "Not *literally,* Eddie!"

"Yes, literally! If that's what it takes! Throughout the week, there will be a series of challenges taking place. Your opponent? *The house of the groom.*"

By the way he's pronouncing the words, drawing out each syllable, you could almost mistake it for *the house of doom.*

"What kind of challenges?" McCall warily questions.

Eddie's devious smirk is anything but comforting. "You'll see soon enough. Thanks to Sheryl, you've all been pre-assigned rooms with your names posted on the doors. Get settled in, and meet me on the sand in thirty minutes sharp."

Malik looks excited. He played nearly every sport in high school before graduating two years ago. He excelled at nearly all of them. "Sounds good, Uncle Eddie."

"Only Eddie, no uncle."

Once the crowd has dispersed, Cole and I walk up the steps and begin to search for our rooms.

Quietly, he says, "Your somewhat excessive aunt and game show host uncle weren't exactly on my list of things to be prepared for."

I smile, but I'm sure it comes out as more of a grimace. To make up for it, I do the worst jazz hands I've ever seen in my life. *"Surprise!"*

"I can't say I'm one to pass up a challenge." He grins.

We struggle to find a door with Cole's name on it, but it shouldn't catch me off-guard. No one knew that Cole was coming… or who *wasn't*. Hung on the door and written in fancy lettering is a list of names: My eight-year-old brother, Ryder, Malik, and… *Jesse*.

Jesse—my original, self-absorbed plus one—the person who somehow led me to be standing in this hallway with Cole.

As I point my finger at Jesse's name, my attempt at a smile turns more into an apologetic glance. "I think I found your room."

Cole bursts out laughing at the irony. "We should've expected it. But this, along with the look on your face… is hilarious, Fin."

I can't help but laugh as well. "We're just getting started, and it's already a hot mess!"

"Do you think people are going to call *me* Jesse?"

My eyes go wide. "Uhh, I hope not. That would be awkward. I'll be sure to let them know."

"I appreciate it," he responds. "At least you found my room. Thanks, Babe," he says sarcastically.

I shudder. "Please don't ever call me that again."

He smiles, knowing *exactly* what he's doing. "Sorry, Babe. No promises."

Chapter 6

HOLD IT TOGETHER

I open the trunk and pull out my large, tan suitcase, watching as it hits the driveway with a *thud*. It doesn't roll well on the walkway, so I jut out my hip to awkwardly carry it. As I make my way to the front door, I leave Cole and Malik outside talking about who knows what. Once inside, I'm able to roll it easily… until I reach the staircase that leads to the second floor.

Bump, I hit the first step. *Bump*, and the second.

"I'm coming, Roomie!" McCall rushes to meet me. She lifts the bottom of my suitcase, allowing us to carry it upstairs with ease.

"Thanks," I say, grateful for her help.

We stop at the door that has *Finley & McCall* on the sign. I glance around the room, taking it all in for the first time. There are two queen beds, each lined with silk sheets and an abundance of throw pillows. There's a tall dresser with accents of gold handles.

McCall's suitcase is sitting open on the ground next to mine, but from the lack of contents inside, I notice that she has already unpacked. I don't take the time to do so. I'll only be here for a week. Living out of a suitcase will work just fine. I don't like putting my laundry away at home, nonetheless on vacation.

I throw myself onto a bed, claiming it as my own. McCall does the same, lying flat on the bed beside me. Despite the sun shining through the window behind her, I notice how her features have changed since December when I last saw her.

Her hair is still brown, yet it's a shade or two lighter. Her skin has the golden tan that it's missing in the winter months. The freckles that she's had since we were kids stand out, a light brown whisper dancing across her perfect nose and high cheekbones.

"So," she starts with a sly grin, "Cole, huh?"

Nervously, I chuckle. "Apparently so. But we don't have time for the details now. We have to meet Eddie on the sand."

"Eddie and his games," she says with a quiet hum.

I still feel bad for keeping secrets, especially from McCall. However, she's the *worst* at keeping them. Not because she likes drama and gossiping but because it would simply eat away at her. More likely than not, she would feel the incessant need to tell someone—*anyone*.

Although I love her to death, I can't have her spilling my secret just after it's begun.

As soon as the wedding is over and we return home, I'll call her. I'll do what I should've done after things ended with Jesse. I'll explain everything—the beginning, the middle, the end. She'll soon know all the events that sent a gut-wrenching pain through me, as well as everything that got me past it.

This place is like our own personal paradise. The house sits on the beach with a large back patio that leads straight to the cool sand and inviting water.

"Over here!" Eddie calls from my right.

As we're walking toward him, I notice the second house—*the groom's house*—that he previously mentioned. We walk until we're in between both houses.

I turn to face Cole, who met me outside on the patio. "Any guesses on what we're doing?"

"I'm stuck between building sandcastles with your siblings or skinny dipping with your grandma," he replies bluntly. Despite his attempt at a poker face, a small grin starts to show.

I laugh before I can contain it. "*Ew*, Cole! That is *not* the mental image I was wanting."

He chuckles, and we turn our focus to Eddie as he begins.

"If you haven't figured it out yet, we're going to be playing America's favorite game!"

Malik excitedly rubs his hands together. *"Clearly, we're going to be playing football."*

"No, not football. We're going to play what *should be* America's favorite game."

Sierra steps up next to Eddie with a glove in her hand. *"Baseball."* On cue, a baseball is tossed to her, and she catches it with ease.

A man with hair so dark that it's nearly black stands next to them, yet I can't quite place who he is. "My personal favorite." As he wraps an arm around Sierra, the familiarity makes sense.

Dalton—Sierra's fiancé and soon-to-be husband. I've only seen pictures of him on social media, although I've seen a *lot* since Sierra is the most Instagram-friendly person I know. Based on his apparent love of sports, he's surely on Eddie's good side.

Eddie starts, "You'll be split into two teams—the Hollow Oak Beach House and the Old Lavender House."

Sierra turns to Dalton with narrowed eyes. "Oh, you're going down!"

He smirks. "May the odds be ever in your favor."

She separates from him and turns to the entirety of Hollow Oak, calling out, "Huddle up!" She signals her hands for us to come close.

Once we form a large circle, Peyton, one of the bridesmaids, speaks up. "I'm definitely out. Sorry,

Sierra, but it's clear that I'll only be cheering everyone on from the sidelines." Her pregnant belly stands out as she's wearing leggings and an oversized t-shirt.

The man standing beside her suggests, "I'll take Peyton's place." He's a groomsman and should technically be on the other team, but due to Peyton's pregnancy, she asked him to stay in the house with her to help with their daughter. By default, he's now on the bride's team. Gratefully so, because we may need all the help we can get.

"Perfect! Anyone else?" Sierra asks.

Chatter flows through our small circle as people agree to play and choose their position. Others, like my mom, opt out completely. After a quick hands-in, we're on the field. In reality, '*the field*' is only the sand.

After tossing around words that are a foreign concept to me, our team consists of Cole pitching, Malik on first base (his high school position), Eddie on second, Blaire (the Maid of Honor) playing short, Sierra on third, Ryder as the catcher, and myself, McCall, and Matt in the outfield.

Those who aren't playing from both households sit on the back patio, cheering us on from their Adirondack chairs. My little sister, Wren, is one of them. She's fifteen and claims that sports have never been her '*thing*'. Truthfully, she's not wrong.

She's playing with Juniper, Peyton and Matt's one-year-old. So far, Juniper is the life of the party.

I turn my attention back to the baseball game as it begins. The glove on my left hand is a little big and shifts uncomfortably. Aside from playing in my backyard, I've never played a real game of baseball—or softball—a day in my life. I guess sports haven't ever been my thing either.

First up to bat and representing the OLH team (the Old Lavender House) is Dalton. Cole stands on the pitcher's mound, and although I can't see his face, the concentration is clear throughout his entire body.

"Come on, Cole!" I cheer. I try to clap, but the troublesome glove gets in my way. Once Dalton is fully in position, Cole throws the ball.

"Strike!" My dad yells from the sidelines. With no other spots available, he settled on being the umpire and promised to be fair. Cole pitches two more times, each accompanied by my dad's voice echoing yet another, "*Strike!*"

"This is rigged!" Dalton chuckles, walking away from home base.

Another guy walks up to bat, yet Cole isn't so lucky this time. Neither am I. On the first pitch, the ball meets the bat with a loud *thunk*. As it soars through the air, nearly everyone in my area starts to run for the ball. My legs ache as I run, struggling to keep up in the sand. My eyes follow the ball until it lands in Matt's glove.

Our small crowd begins to cheer.

Almost an hour passes before our game comes to a close. The final score is six to four, and the winning team is… the HOBH team. Though I can't say I contributed too much toward the score, others on our team did great. Cole and Malik were by far our star players, which wasn't too surprising.

Cole never really consistently played any sport growing up, but he was usually exceptional at whatever he did. Even with carefree games of tag, he consistently won. *It was infuriating.* Luckily, I'm on the same team as him now—the *winning* team.

Eddie, still ecstatic over our win, calls out to the crowd, "I've worked up an appetite! Who's up for dinner? I have the perfect place in mind."

With my stomach growling, I want to cheer even louder now than I did when Cole scored a home run.

Cole and I drive together to the restaurant, which is only a short, four-minute drive from the house.

"Wow, Fin! This is going to be our first real outing as a couple," he jokingly points out as we turn down the road that leads to the restaurant.

"That's such a weird sentence. A *couple*?"

"Don't blame me!" Cole laughs. "You were the mastermind in this whole ordeal."

"Yeah, I know." I pause. "Do you think it's believable so far?"

He shrugs. "I don't know. We haven't done anything super *couple-y*."

"*Couple-y?*" I mock.

"You know what I mean. There's nothing too *romantic* about playing baseball."

I relax against the passenger seat with the glovebox now in my line of sight. It jogs my memory of the old, withered receipt with our rules. "Should we hold hands?"

"Say *what?*" Cole remarks.

"You heard me. It *is* a rule, after all. We should hold hands as we walk in. It would be helpful to keep up our *lovey-dovey* appearance."

He nods, parking the car. "If we have to."

"Should we practice before we get out?"

"*Practice? Finley!* You had this whole idea of us, and you seriously want to *practice* holding my hand?" He laughs, dumbfoundedly running his hands through his brown hair as he turns to face me. "That's a little ridiculous."

"No, it's not!" I protest. "I've never held your hand before. It'll probably make me laugh."

"*Laugh?* Why on Earth would holding my hand be funny?"

"Because it's so uncomfortable! You know I laugh in weird situations, so I'm sure I would break our cover."

"I don't know why I'm agreeing to this," he says, shaking his head with a smile. He quietly chuckles to himself as he continues. "Honestly, I'm not sure why I agreed to *any* of this. Here." He outstretches his palm, holding it open over the gearshift.

I place my hand over his, yet I'm hesitant to let them touch. My hand hovers with a mere two inches separating mine from his.

"Oh, come on, Fin," he exclaims with a white-toothed grin. In an instant, he reaches his hand up to grab mine, making our fingers intertwine.

I bite the inside of my cheeks so I *don't* laugh.

"Okay, not bad. I think I'll be fine."

After a brief moment of his eyes on mine, Cole releases my hand. "Now let's go, Sweetie. We have a dinner to attend."

"Ew! Why '*Sweetie*'?" I grimace.

"Finley, are you forgetting this is supposed to be a *relationship*?" he teases. "People normally have cute nicknames."

"Correction," I pause, lifting a finger. "*Slightly creepy* and *weird* nicknames are not *cute*. Maybe it works in books and movies, but I don't know about them in real life. In all the years I spent with Jesse, we didn't have a *single* nickname for one another."

Jokingly, he says, "Well, maybe that's why you and Jesse didn't last. You never called him your Sweet Honey Pie."

"Maybe I didn't call him that because I'm not his *ninety-year-old grandmother*."

"I mean…" he starts before I cut him off.

"And I'm not yours either, so don't expect a nickname."

"Yes, ma'am," he says with wide eyes.

I open the car door and hop outside. I grin at his remarks. There's something about Cole that always makes me smile, even in moments when I wish I could suppress it to prove a point.

Naturally—or at least as naturally as I can—I take his hand. "Don't embarrass me in here," I order.

"No problem. You'll embarrass yourself enough all on your own, Buttercup."

I notice McCall in the parking lot. Once her eyes meet mine... I start to chuckle.

Cole turns to me. "Everything good?"

"Mm-hmm," I nod, tight-lipped and refusing to let another giggle escape.

Now is *not* the time for my childishness. I had a boyfriend for over three years. I should easily be able to hold the hand of someone I have no romantic feelings for without giggling like a little schoolgirl.

"It's because I'm holding your hand, isn't it?"

With my mouth sealed, the bubbling laughter grows. "*Mm-hmm*," I manage.

He squeezes my hand a little tighter. "Hold it together, Sunshine."

I do the complete *opposite*.

SUNDAY *playlist*

- Summerland —————————————— half-alive
- Lover ————————————————— Taylor Swift
- Ex's & Oh's ————————————— Elle King
- Telling Myself ————————— Joshua Bassett
- Float —————————————— HARBOUR
- I Ain't Worried ————————— OneRepublic
- Sunrise, Sunburn, Sunset ————— Luke Bryan
- I Want You ——————————— Sun Room
- BRIGHTSIDE ——————— The Lumineers
- Daydreaming ————————— Harry Styles
- Cruel Summer ——————— Taylor Swift
- The Tide ——————————— Niall Horan
- stuck on us ——— Claire Rosinkranz, Aidan Bissett
- Feel Something ——————— Joshua Bassett
- Swim (Reprise) ————————————— Valley
- Dog Days Are Over —— Florence + The Machine

Chapter 7

CHEF'S KISS

It's barely 7:45 in the morning, and everyone is standing outside on the perfectly manicured lawn. Even though we did our best last night to get Eddie to spill the beans, we've still been kept in the dark about today's plans.

The sun shines over the horizon, casting a yellow shadow over the small crowd of people. The early morning seems to affect everyone differently.

Cole stands next to me, dressed for the day in khaki shorts and a t-shirt. He is naturally an early riser, whereas I enjoy sleeping in. When carpooling to school, he often had his music blaring before I was fully functioning.

Eddie is even more bright-eyed than Cole. "Good morning, everyone!"

A slow chorus of, "Good morning," is called out in unison. Aunt Sheryl's words stand out in the sea of voices, extra peppy thanks to today's *second* mug of coffee in her hand.

Eddie continues with a lengthy explanation. All week, the houses will be competing head-to-head in a cook-off. I'm starving, so I hope there are some secret chefs among us. He has two bowls, both of which are filled with folded strands of paper.

"We will draw names from each bowl to see who will be the first to show off their cooking skills. One bowl represents the house of the bride, the other the house of the groom."

It's almost as if the reaping from *The Hunger Games* has turned into a reality cooking show.

Dalton pipes up, "For breakfast today, two lucky members of each house will be making French toast."

A man steps forward, and I assume he's Dalton's father based on their splitting imagery. "From the house of the groom…" he announces as he reaches into the first bowl and pulls out a strand of paper. "Jacob and Paris."

Their names don't ring a bell to me and neither do the faces of the two people who cheer with delight. They must know how to make some killer French toast.

It's now Eddie's turn to choose. "And from the house of the bride…."

I say a silent prayer that it's *not* me. Hopefully, due to the sheer amount of names in the bowl, my name won't be drawn at all this week.

"Malik and McCall."

As McCall stands frozen, Malik shouts out, "Let's go!"

She turns to me, whispering, "I hope Malik can mix up something other than his nasty protein shakes."

Malik takes control in the kitchen by setting out the proper utensils, combining the ingredients into a mixing bowl, and dipping the bread into the batter.

He gives McCall one job—to make sure nothing burns. *In the nicest way possible,* McCall is admittedly awful at it.

The first batch is now scorching the inside of the trash can. For the time being, McCall's new job is to silence the smoke alarm that is crying out for help. Despite her best efforts of repeatedly waving a dish towel in the air, the smoke alarm's beeping remains constant and *loud.* According to Sierra, it went haywire yesterday during lunch when nothing was smoking… but there is definitely a burning essence in the air now.

As they shuffle around the kitchen, McCall and Malik's audience consists of Cole, Sierra, Aunt Kira, my mom, Eddie, and myself. If any of us try to help or assist them in any way, they'll be disqualified. Even though I'm silently glad my name wasn't picked, I wish I could do *something* to help.

Malik is mixing more batter while McCall stands at the stove, anxiously waiting for the right time to flip the slices of bread. The smoke alarm hasn't let up, so she spends even more time frantically waving the towel in the air.

To make matters worse—*yet comedically making them better*—Eddie grabs an extra whisk and is now speaking into it with the tone of a game show host. "Oh no! This toast is *toast*, folks! We're on our third attempt now. Will McCall accomplish the desired look? Drumroll please!"

We all drumroll from the kitchen island, adding to the *unnecessary, yet entertaining* suspense.

"The drumroll is *not* helping!" McCall expresses as she rushes back to the stove. She flips over the bread and sure enough… it's singed, similar to the trashcan toast.

"*Not again!*" Eddie cries out.

Malik temporarily stops cracking eggs for the batter and turns to face the third failed endeavor. "*Goodness*, McCall! How are you still burning it?"

"I don't know! I'm not used to this stove!" So quiet it's hardly audible, she adds in, "…or really *any* stove."

"What is the burner set to?" Malik shouts over the incessant beeping.

McCall grabs the white hand towel yet again, attempting to stop the beeping. I'm beginning to wonder if Dalton's family has sabotaged our smoke alarm. She leans in closer to the dial to inspect it. "I don't have my contacts in. I can't tell!"

Malik walks over to look for himself. Once he sees what the burner is set on, his mouth drops. "No wonder you're burning them!" He lowers the temperature and removes the pan to cool down.

The whisk is raised to Eddie's mouth, once again serving as his microphone. He gives us a play-by-play as if we're not sitting beside him. "Well, would you look at that, folks! Malik thinks he's found a solution! Will it work? Tune in later to find out!"

With the burner slightly cooled, McCall sets a new slice into the pan. For her self-esteem—and for the sake of my growling stomach—I hope the fourth time's a charm.

We're standing back outside as we wait for the grand reveal. A table is set in the open grass between the houses with two covered, silver platters in the middle.

"3! 2! 1…" everyone chants. On the final count, the covers are lifted and both dishes are revealed.

Once the stovetop situation was settled and they learned to ignore the smoke alarm, McCall and Malik got into the groove of things. The next batches were cooked to perfection, and they look delicious.

To make up for her mishaps, McCall went the extra mile when plating the food by strategically placing strawberries on the stack of French toast. She found powdered sugar in the very back of the pantry and sprinkled it around the plate with hopes that it isn't expired.

From the groom's team, Jacob and Paris' attempt looks amazing as well, although they're missing the extra details in the presentation.

Eddie authorizes a taste test, inviting Aunt Sheryl and the groom's parents to dive in and help with the judging.

Cole nudges me with his shoulder, leaning in closer. "McCall looks pretty stressed over there."

I follow his line of sight toward her. In the five seconds that I've been watching, she's already fiddled with her ponytail and straightened her necklace on countless occasions. "Oh, she does," I grimace. "I'll be back."

As I'm on my way over, Eddie begins. "The votes are in!"

"You good?" I ask McCall.

Eddie continues. "After breaking down the taste and presentation, we've decided that..."

"Yeah, just a little nervous after I—" McCall's sentence is cut short.

"Although both parties presented a flavorsome dish, Malik and McCall are the winners!"

As the Hollow Oak household cheers, the expression that spreads across McCall's face is one of pure shock, excitement, and perhaps most of all—*relief.*

McCall blows a quick chef's kiss to both sets of parents. "Thank you, thank you!" she exclaims.

Malik comes over with his hand raised for a high-five. "We won, and we didn't set anything on fire!"

McCall smiles, giving him a high-five. "Thank goodness! I wouldn't want to see Aunt Sheryl's reaction to *that*."

Chapter 8

LOVER

The next hour in the Hollow Oak Beach House feels much calmer. Cole and I sit at the table in front of the giant bay window, glancing out at the beach view. I hold a deck of cards in my hands, shuffling them.

In our nook, it feels as if we're in our own private world of one-way glass. We're still connected to the rest of the house and getting a front-row seat to the entertainment, yet no one is paying any attention to us. Aunt Sheryl pours her third cup of coffee, Malik goes on a run, Juniper giggles as one of the bridesmaids, Caroline, is playing with her, and Grandma Rose yells out crossword puzzle questions, only to wait for someone else to shout back with an answer.

I place the cards on the table, straightening them after being shuffled. "What do you want to play?"

"Speed?" Cole suggests.

"Sounds good to me."

He gives me a pleading look. I distinctly remember it from when we were kids trying to decide which movie to watch. He *always* wanted superheroes and sports, and I *always* wanted princesses in frilly dresses. "Will I at least get to shuffle after this game?"

Chuckling, I say, "That depends if you win or lose."

"We've only been here a day, and you're turning into Eddie." He smiles.

"Oh *please*," I scoff. "We've been arguing over who gets to deal the cards since we were seven."

It's true. Every Wednesday night for as long as I can remember, we've gone to the Baxter household for Game Night. This varied from dice games, Jenga, and every game in between.

Capital *G*, capital *N*—*Game Night* has become so engrained into our weekly schedules that my mom no longer adds it to our family calendar. Over the past few years, I've occasionally been absent. More often than not, Jesse was the reason. He'd tell me to use the lack of family scheduling as an excuse more times than I'd like to admit.

I'd want to go to dinner, or he'd want us to go hang out with his friends. Some weeks, we would go to the drive-in to rewatch 90s movies from the front seats of his truck.

Vividly, a memory flashes into my mind from last December. It was the week before Christmas, and the drive-in was playing *Home Alone*. Right as the robbers broke into the house and set off every booby trap that young Kevin had set up, my phone dinged.

It was Cole, asking where I was and stating that everyone was missing me that night. He sent another message a few minutes later. This one was a picture of his younger sister, Cassie, cheesing next to a towering stack of Jenga blocks. She never liked the *actual* game but always wanted to see how high she could stack them. Based on the picture, this was her most impressive tower yet!

I smiled when I saw it and quietly blew a huff of air from my nose. I replied that I was at the drive-in and beyond impressed by her tower.

Jesse leaned over the center console, sneaking a glance at my phone. "Who are you texting?" He tried to ask it nonchalantly, but the expression on his face and his furrowed brows made him look more serious.

"Cole," I hesitantly responded as I shut my phone off.

Jesse looked ready to explode before I quickly pointed out, "It's Wednesday's Game Night. They were wondering where I was, and he sent me a picture of Cassie."

"*Oh.*" For some reason, the word sounded hard coming out of his mouth. Finally, he spoke up again. "Who is Cassie? His girlfriend?"

I pursed my lips together and did my best to hide my slight annoyance. "No, he doesn't have a girlfriend. They broke up over the summer. Cassie's his little sister, remember?"

"Doesn't ring a bell."

At this point, Jesse and I had been dating for over two and a half years. With how close Cole's family was with mine, Cassie was almost always at my house. She was over every weekend for sure, playing with Ryder and Saylor. Jesse hadn't just seen her, *but he had met her* on numerous occasions. The fact that he had no recollection of her sent a slight chill down my spine.

"Well, can we just watch the movie?" Jesse asked.

"Yeah, sorry."

I had just watched Home Alone a few weeks prior as we set up our Christmas tree, but Jesse insisted on coming here. He argued that the movie was a classic, saying I could watch it more than once a year. After all, it was *his* favorite.

Following the conversation we had about my text messages with Cole, Jesse and I hardly said another word on the ride home. I told him goodbye as we pulled into my driveway, and he gave me a halfhearted peck as a farewell.

After that night, I told myself I would consistently attend Game Night. Call it bad luck, or maybe it was purposeful… but Jesse seemed to keep me busy every Wednesday night. Whether it was excuses to stay at his house later than expected or him getting distracted in a random store, I missed the beginning, the middle, and sometimes even the end of Game Night every single week.

Since the breakup, I haven't missed one yet.

Cole waves a hand in front of my face now, bringing me back to reality. *"Hellooo?* Earth to Finley," he echoes.

I jolt, leaving the apparent trance I was in.

"You good?" He chuckles, teeth showing through his smile.

"Yeah, just thinking. Sorry."

"Nah, no need to apologize. Just don't give me a reason to revoke your card dealer privileges."

I laugh, feeling the slight bounce in my shoulders. After a moment I say, "I feel bad for missing so many Game Nights."

"Eh, no worries. We can make up for lost time now." He grins softly.

Reminiscing on some of the rough patches with Jesse brought me back to those cold, winter months. Yet now as I see Cole's smile, I feel the warmth come back into my chest.

"Question!" Grandma Rose calls from the couch. "Does anyone know a five-letter word for a very close friend? Unless I've messed up the rest of this crossword puzzle, the second letter is *O* and the fourth is *E*."

The first word—or rather name—that pops into my head is *Cole*. But it's only four letters and is obviously not going to be the correct answer, so I don't dare say it aloud.

"*Lover*?" Sierra offers.

"Yes, dear! That has to be the one," my grandma exclaims. With satisfaction, she repeats it quietly to herself. "A very close friend, a *lover*."

I deal the cards for the game of *Speed*, giving Cole his hand. A knock sounds at the front door, followed by Dalton walking inside just moments later.

The smile in Sierra's voice is audible through her tone. "Speaking of a lover." She rises from the couch to meet him.

He pulls his hand from behind his back, exposing the large bouquet of roses.

"Oh, how sweet!" Grandma Rose cheers. "What a gentleman!"

Sierra takes the flowers and gives Dalton a quick kiss. "Thanks, Babe."

Cole's foot quickly taps mine beneath the table. "*See!*" he whispers, but it comes out like a snake trying to hiss. "*I told you* people have cute nicknames. She just called him *Babe*."

I chuckle. "Look at you, such a little expert on love!"

"I mean I've tried—and failed—my fair share of relationships, but *they* seem to have it figured out." He motions to Sierra and Dalton. "Maybe we need to take notes. Where's your receipt when we need it?"

I have to hold in a laugh, yet a smile still escapes.

We play a fast game of Speed—*hence the name*—and Cole wins. It doesn't come as a shock to either of us. In fact, that's probably why he let me shuffle the cards first. He knew I wouldn't be doing it again.

As the cards mix together between his hands, I watch the bride and groom. As Cole would say, I'm taking notes. She takes the bouquet from its packaging, fills a vase with water from the sink, and places the flowers inside. The petals are white and have different hues of purple—the wedding colors.

"Rule #6," I start, referring to the rules we made yesterday on our drive to Sunrise Beach. "Don't bring me flowers."

"Ah, a late addition," Cole remarks. "Why can I not bring you flowers?"

I shrug. "It's just too symbolic."

He leans in closer, careful not to be overheard as he continues. "So, *you* have this elaborate idea to bring me here and be your boyfriend... but if I bring you something that grows from the ground—a literal *weed* if you think about it—it's too much?" He doesn't hold in his quiet laugh.

I sigh dramatically, thinking of the best way to explain this. "It's more than a *weed.* It has meaning."

He raises a single eyebrow.

Reluctantly, I continue. "I'm a sucker for florals, okay? I think I could even fall in love with Otto Jones in his vomit-green Heelys if he brought me flowers."

"Wow, Fin. That's a little alarming."

"Okay, maybe that was a *slight* exaggeration," I begin. "But flowers truly are my weakness—my curse from a wicked witch, my fatal flaw, my kryptonite...."

Cole nods, the gears turning in his head. "So, I bring you flowers, and you fall in love with me? Note taken."

I chuckle as I point my finger at him. "Don't be a rule-breaker, Baxter."

He smiles as he hands me my cards for the rematch I'll inevitably lose. "I won't make any promises that I can't keep."

a very close
friend, a _lover_.

Chapter 9

FEELS LIKE FATE

"I'm sorry, but I have to ask," McCall begins.

"Ask what exactly?" I question warily, raising my eyebrows.

Shortly after the flower situation, McCall and I decide to take a walk, exploring the small town and quaint shops.

McCall continues, now asking the question I've been wanting to avoid. "What happened between you and Jesse? Y'all were together for so long."

I pause for a moment. "We just weren't going to work out in the end, you know?" I sigh. "We were bound to end eventually with us going to different colleges and a... *plethora of other things.*" I don't mention the fact that he cheated on me.

"I get that. People grow apart."

I nod, unsure of how to respond.

"So... Cole, huh?"

It's hard to get past the irony of the old topics I'm having to avoid—*Jesse*, and the new topics I 100% brought upon myself—*Cole*. A small chuckle escapes me. "Who would've guessed... *Cole*."

Saying his name and almost comparing him to Jesse feels wrong. They've always been two separate entities in my life. My *boyfriend*—no spaces—and my *boy friend*—boy, *space*, friend. The space still stands between us, yet we're having to pretend as if the small gap has closed.

"How did *that* happen?" she asks as we walk into a small boutique.

"Welcome in!" The girl behind the counter exclaims with a wide grin.

I smile back at the girl, calling out a polite, "Hi." I've been looking for a new pair of jean shorts, so I head to the rack lined with denim on gold hangers. I turn back to face McCall. "Cole and I just kind of... happened. It was pretty fast honestly." *Very fast, in fact.* It was barely forty-eight hours ago.

McCall smiles proudly. "Years ago, I had an inkling that you two would end up together. Looks like I was right all along."

I quietly chuckle.

"Seriously though, you and Cole getting together after all these years? It kind of feels like fate."

"Fate seems like a *bit* much. Besides, what makes you think we're destined to be together?"

"There's a multitude of reasons. You've been close to each other since birth—literally *and* geographically, your moms are best friends, and you grew up living next to each other. If you think about your story on paper, you can't tell me that doesn't sound like the plot of a romance novel."

I shoot her a playful glare. "I think that just means we've read one too many romance novels."

She grabs a light blue dress from another rack and holds it up against her. "Maybe he's been secretly in love with you since elementary school."

"Most definitely not. He's had his fair share of girlfriends and situationships over the years. There's no way he's been in love with me."

"Well, he seems to be in love with you now."

At her comment, I pause. Just for a moment, I forgot about the front I'm supposed to uphold. I forgot that in her mind, Cole and I really *are* more than friends.

So, even though Cole is not *actually* in love with me, I say, "Sure."

Apparently—*admittedly*—that's the wrong answer.

"Sure? What kind of response is *sure*?" McCall chuckles, placing the blue dress back on the rack and reaching for a pink shirt. "Have you said *I love you* to each other?"

"Easy now, killer." After having no luck in the jean department, I try on a pair of funky sunglasses and glance in the mirror. These are definitely not my style. "We haven't been dating *that* long." *Zero days in reality.*

"Okay, okay. I'll stop prying." She lifts her arms in surrender. "However, if the day comes... I'd love a front-row seat to the next family wedding."

"You sound a little *too* much like my mom."

She continues, ignoring my comment. "Actually, maybe not front row. I would love to be another bridesmaid... possibly the Maid of Honor?"

I laugh. "I'll see what I can do."

After not buying anything—*with the money we don't have*—we walk out of the boutique.

The bell hanging above the door chimes in sync with McCall's phone. She glances down as we walk past the hanging flower pots that line the strip of boutiques and small businesses.

"Do you like horses?" she asks.

I furrow my brows at the sudden topic switch. "Umm... yeah. I guess so. What about them?"

She gives me the full explanation that I needed the first time. "Sierra texted. They're making plans to go horseback riding. Do you want to go?"

"Oh, that sounds like fun! I hope we make it back to the house in time."

Chapter 10

OUR STORY

After McCall and I return, I hurry inside to find the tennis shoes that I packed. We have fifteen minutes before we leave to go horseback riding.

As I reach for my bedroom doorknob, a hand grabs mine and lightly tugs me back. A small "*Oh!*" escapes me with shock.

"*SOS!*" Cole whisper-yells, still holding onto my hand.

"Hello to you too," I joke.

He leads me through the long hallway of closed bedroom doors, stopping in front of a door smaller than the rest and without anyone's name. I assume it's a linen closet or something of the sort. Cole opens the door, revealing a narrow ladder that leads straight *up*. It's dark in the small area and only wide enough for us to fit in a single file line. Hollow Oak is an old manor, so the strange space is unique and unlike anything I've ever seen before. He releases my hand and begins to climb the ladder.

With what seems like no choice, I follow him. Maybe my curiosity has gotten the best of me since the only thing he has said is *SOS*.

In the dark, I climb up each rung and take a wild guess on my footing and hand placements. We finally reach the top. I hear a quiet click that is followed by a bright light filtering in from the sky above us.

"What the…" I mutter.

Cole climbs out first, offering me his hand. With the blue sky shining into the enclosed space, I can now see how high up we've climbed. I'm not necessarily afraid of heights, but falling down a secret chute is definitely not on my agenda for this week. For fear of falling, I take his hand.

"Thanks," I mutter as he helps guide me onto the roof. "What are we doing up here? How did you even find this? Have you been sneaking around the house?"

"Whoa, one question at a time." Cole smiles. "I found this spot because you left me alone with your family for an hour. I couldn't find your dad, and Malik was still on a run, so I was surrounded by women. In the nicest way possible—your family is *crazy*."

I don't even need context at this point. Laughing, I say, "Tell me something I don't know. But for clarification, are you talking about *one* crazy person in particular?"

He lets out a deep breath like this could take a while. "Your Aunt Sheryl probably wins the number one award for crazy. After asking about my life story, she trusted me to help choose the centerpiece design. For crying out loud, she hardly knows me! Yet there I was, choosing between different types of silk ribbons."

"Aww, she must like you!" Aunt Sheryl wanting help is like a right of passage. She rarely asks for anyone's opinion, and she typically only listens to her own. The centerpiece question could've been a test in some unexplainable way, but I don't point this out to him.

"Your Grandma Rose is *very* persistent as well. I had no clue how to answer any of their questions!"

"What were they asking you?" I take in the bird's eye view of the beach.

"All of the nosey relationship questions!" He chuckles. "How we met, how long we've been together…."

"Okay, how did you answer them?"

"I tried to avoid them like the plague."

"Cole, you can't *not* answer the questions. That's practically *Fake Dating 101*! They're going to think we're an awful couple."

"No, don't worry. I answered a few but steered clear of most of their questions like a *pro*." He reaches into his pocket and pulls out his phone. "I have an alarm set to go off every six minutes to answer a fake phone call. *Genius*! Right?"

I place a hand over my mouth, stifling a laugh. "That's so weird, Cole. They're probably onto you."

"I pretended to be talking to my mom and dad. I would've answered all their questions if I knew *how*. We made a list of rules... but no details about our *'story'*." He makes quotation marks in the air. "That's what your family members want—*the juicy stuff*. Who actually knows what happened between you and Jesse?"

"Well..." I grit my teeth, drawing in a sharp breath. "No one knows anything. I just told McCall that the breakup with Jesse was mutual, but that's about it."

"So, I showed up as your boyfriend while they were still expecting him?"

"I know, it's awful! But what was I supposed to do?" I frantically wave my hands around. "Text everyone, saying, *'Hey, my boyfriend cheated on me'*?"

"Not at all. Things would really be awkward then." We sit in silence until the sound of a ringtone fills the air. Cole fumbles for his phone as I see the alarm going off on the screen. "Sorry, I have to take this... just kidding."

I shake my head as I notice the time. Everyone will be leaving shortly.

"So," he begins, "What's our story?"

With the time crunch, I respond quickly. "We've obviously known each other our whole lives." I think back to my conversation with McCall and her thoughts on our *'fated relationship'*. "If anyone asks, you can tell them that Jesse and I mutually broke up. For the sake of my ego, let's leave out the cheating. You and I started dating pretty recently. It's hard to put a date on it since we instantaneously fell head over heels. Our first date was a picnic on the lake, and our first kiss was after an ice cream date at Bertha's. Sound good?"

"Sounds perfect, Babe." A mischievous grin flashes across his face with the last word.

I shoot him a glare at the nickname and head back to the opening that leads inside.

He smirks before continuing. "Now I'm prepared to gossip about us with your grandma."

I sarcastically exclaim, "Get on her good side, and maybe she'll let you paint her toenails to prep for the wedding."

Cole grimaces. "Eww! That's not a good mental image there, Fin."

Now it's my turn for a mischievous grin. "Sorry, not sorry... *Babe*." I relish in the moment, taking in the defeated expression on Cole's face before disappearing down the chute.

Before I'm left behind, I rush frantically to put on my tennis shoes. I find them buried at the very bottom of my suitcase. It is stuffed with clothes and personal belongings, everything I'll need for the next week, yet I can't help but feel as if I've forgotten something. I slip on my socks and shoes and sprint out the front door.

"I'm coming, I'm coming!" I shout as everyone gets into their cars. Cole stands next to the SUV that

Malik just climbed into, and he's holding the car door for me.

The instructors at the horseback riding facility coax us into learning the ropes—*literally*. We're taught the basics, and we review the route before going on our way. It's going to be a mile-long ride as we navigate the horses through a trail in the woods.

We stand in an open area with a horse stationed beside each of us. Everyone is eighteen and older, except for my sister, Wren. The rules state that all minors must wear a safety helmet, which makes her feel slightly singled out.

"This is so embarrassing," Wren mutters under her breath.

Sierra sympathetically gives her a pat on the back. "Only three more years."

McCall reassuringly exclaims, "It doesn't look as bad as you think!"

"At least it's your favorite color," I call out.

"I don't see any of you wearing one," Wren points out with sass coating her tone.

Truthfully, she does have a point.

"Alrighty!" Our instructor, a thirty-something-year-old man with a thick country accent starts. "Is everyone ready?"

Cole quickly walks over to him. He talks expressively with his hands, yet he's not loud enough for anyone else to hear.

Our instructor nods, listening intently. "Ah, I see." He turns to face the rest of us. "Gimme a sec. You can all carefully mount your horses now!"

Cole walks over to me.

"What was that about?" I ask him, motioning to the instructor.

"You'll see." He smiles. "Need a hand?"

My horse is pretty tall, so I accept his offer. Cole bends down, cradling his hands so I can use them to boost myself up. I step up and swing my other leg over the horse as a strand of my blonde hair swoops in front of my eyes. I tuck it behind my ear and express a quiet, "Thank you," to Cole.

The instructor returns with a helmet in hand. He outstretches it to Cole. "This one should work."

Cole proudly places it on his head, and it flattens the waves in his brown hair. "Perfect. Thank you, sir." After he walks over and mounts his horse, he turns to face Wren.

She laughs. "I knew I always liked you for a reason."

Silently, I think to myself, *that makes two of us.*

Chapter 11

SUN TO STARS

Our time spent horseback riding was therapeutic, but we made the mistake of skipping lunch. Cole and I now sit in the kitchen at Hollow Oak as we finish getting a bite to eat.

From the large window, I notice the sun is beginning to set. The rays meet the horizon with a multitude of orange and pink hues.

"Beach sunsets are my favorite," I mention as I take my last bite.

"Let's go outside," he suggests.

I nod eagerly.

A group of people are swimming in the water as their dark silhouettes contrast against the sky. I hear Sierra and Malik through snippets of the loud conversation. Most of the older generation sits on the back patio, fully immersed in adult conversation.

Cole and I have apparently been missing out on all the fun. "Wanna join them?" he asks, nodding to the ocean. The sun bounces off the water, an inviting sight.

"I…" I pause for a moment, ridiculously thinking about how awful my hair will look after getting wet. I shouldn't care about something so silly—or how it will ruin my washing routine. "Yeah, we should."

He slides off his sandals in the sand and begins to empty his pockets.

"Okay, let me go put on a swimsuit, and I'll be —" I turn to face the house when Cole grabs my hand. This seems to be a reoccurring theme.

"Do you have anything in your pockets?" he asks.

Confused, I tilt my head. "Well, no but…"

"But what?" He lifts his other hand and tries to unclasp the watch from my wrist.

"What are you doing?"

"Going for a swim," he says as we're nearing the water.

"Don't you dare," I protest.

"Ah, you'll be fine." He pulls me closer to the ocean.

I feel my watch unclasp and fall to the sand. "Cole!" I laugh.

"Come on, Finley!" The corners of his mouth are upturned into a smile. "The sun is setting, and there's no time to change before it goes down."

My hair is blowing in front of my face as my feet drag in the sand. Now, even if it's occasionally in my way, I usually wear my hair down. Jesse preferred it pulled back, claiming that he liked when my face was fully on display. Call it an act of defiance, but letting my hair flow freely has been one of the ways I've taken the power back into my own hands since our breakup.

Cole lets go of my hand. "It looks like you've given me no choice."

"Thank you," I exhale, out of breath. "Give me two seconds, and I'll be back." Cole stands still, and I begin to walk back toward the house.

Barely above a whisper, I hear his words behind me. "One... two... *time's up!*"

I've hardly taken five steps in the opposite direction before a scream escapes me. Cole's arms wrap around my stomach, and both my feet lift from the cool sand. I let out a quick, alarmed screech.

He laughs, readjusting me so I drape over the top of his shoulder.

I squirm around through bursts of laughter, yet he still manages to carry me. As my feet dangle in the air, my sandals ungracefully hit the sand one by one. I feel every step Cole takes as his shoulder presses into my stomach.

Similar to the summer breeze, our speed picks up as we reach the waves. I yelp as he sets me down into the water. My entire body tenses as it acclimates to the temperature.

Now soaked, I glare up and slightly lift my head in an attempt to close the minor height gap between us. "Was that really necessary?" I question.

"*Definitely,*" Cole says, even though he is just as soaked, and his white shirt is filled with a giant air bubble.

Cheers echo from the water. "Come join us!" Sierra calls.

Cole steps closer to me beneath the waves, shifting our bodies until his back is to the crowd and I'm facing him. "I think I just gained us some relationship points."

I glance around to the patio to see our audience laughing and doing a not-so-sly job of pointing in our direction.

"A little embarrassing for me, but I'm glad I could take one for the team." I give him a stern, business-like pat on the back as I lean in for a fake hug. I pull him down into the water as a little payback.

Cole chuckles, and I can't help but do the same.

We swim over to the group in the water, and I take in my surroundings. The sun's longing rays take their *one last hurrah* for the night before the stars and midnight sky take their place.

Aunt Kira brought out a beach ball lined with LED lights. Deciding to play girls versus guys, we split into two teams in the water. Eddie would be more than satisfied with Sierra's competitive spirit, although a simple game of hit-ball was a little more difficult for

Cole and me in our wet t-shirts. After missing his second play in a row, he took his off and tossed it onto the shore.

After the girls won four out of five games and gloated about our winnings, we call it a night. We couldn't give the guys the satisfaction of catching up and possibly beating us.

Cole, McCall, and I are the last ones to get out of the water. There are only so many showers available, so we don't rush to be the first ones inside—although hot water would be nice.

McCall grabs her belongings from their *convenient* spot on the Adirondack chair. Unlike her, we —*cough, cough: Cole*—weren't as smart with our things. In the fiasco of us getting into the water, we have everything scattered amongst the sand. McCall and I both bundle up in her beach towel, shivering against the breeze that has only gotten cooler in the wake of the sun.

Within a few minutes, Cole manages to locate everything he left in the sand. I, on the other hand, don't have as much luck. Using the flashlights from their phones, we quickly spot my shoes. The only other thing that I had on me was my watch. The small black band sits somewhere in the sand, yet it feels impossible to find.

In our search party of three, we scour the beach. "We'll find it, Fin," Cole reassures me. "If not tonight, then surely tomorrow."

McCall chuckles. "Who knows, maybe Eddie has a metal detector."

"Or Aunt Sheryl," I joke. "Her purse is always *loaded*." Bandaids, miniature scissors, a compact hairbrush that also doubles as a mirror, the mass-market paperback she's currently reading... you name it, and I'm sure Aunt Sheryl more than likely has one in her Mary Poppins bag.

"I'll be right back," Cole says. "I'm going to look for a flashlight that's hopefully brighter than my phone." He walks up to me, grabs the sandals from my hand, and takes them inside.

After Cole walks through the back door, McCall smiles. "Geez, you two are seriously so cute together. It's honestly a little sickening."

I let out a harsh, "*Ha!*" before remembering that she's *not* joking. *I have to get my act together!* "What makes you say that?" I recover.

"Are you kidding?" She smiles from beside me, still wrapped in the same towel. "Finley, he just brought your shoes in so you don't have to hold them. He also carried you into the ocean for crying out loud."

A blush rises in my cheeks as I smile. I have to admit that Cole *is* sweet. Come to think of it, maybe he always has been. After all, he wore a helmet on a horse so Wren didn't feel singled out, he let me step in his hands while being unsure if I had unknowingly stepped in manure, and he allowed me to practice holding his hand so I could feel a tad more comfortable.

In an attempt to rationalize things, I say, "He carried me into the ocean because I wouldn't let him *drag* me... but maybe you do have a point."

"Oh, I *know* I have a point. Now let's pick a new topic. I'm too single for this one."

I smile and resist the urge to say, *me too*. Instead, I try to start a conversation that doesn't involve talking about me or my relationship. "So, how has—"

"I found it!" McCall cheers, cutting me off.

Sure enough, my watch peaks through the sand, just barely visible. She bends down to pick it up, and the shared towel around us almost sends me to the ground as well.

As she's brushing off the excess sand, Cole comes back outside with a flashlight. "I found one!" He turns it on, illuminating a much wider surface area.

"No need!" I call back.

"I found the watch!" McCall shouts.

Walking off the patio and into the sand, Cole starts, "Oh! In that case, I guess I won't be needing th— *Stop*!" He pushes his hand out to us. "*Don't. Move.*"

Chapter 12

DON'T MOVE

"Don't move," Cole repeats.

Other than our occasional shiver, McCall and I stand frozen and confused.

"Why can't we move?" I question frantically.

Cole says nothing, but I follow his gaze… to a possum. It's about twenty feet away from the house and even closer to McCall and me. The possum stares intently at Cole and begins to hiss. Cole stares back, making this the *weirdest* staring contest I've ever witnessed.

McCall squints. "What *is* that? A raccoon?"

"No," I grimace. "It's a possum."

"Ew! That's worse." Without her contacts in, she can only make out its shape. Her poor eyesight makes it even more shocking that she was the one who found my watch in the dark.

"Cole!" I exclaim in a whisper. "What are we going to do? I mean—what are *you* going to do?"

"I don't know yet!" He panics, waving the flashlight in his hand. Without the brighter light, I'm not sure any of us would've spotted the possum until it got too close for comfort. "What am I *supposed* to do?"

"I have no clue! I don't typically have possum encounters."

McCall suggests, "Just try to run it off!"

The possum doesn't stop staring. Cole takes off without another thought and races toward it. "*Shoo, shoo!*"

Instead of shooing, it drops to the ground with a *thud*—playing dead, I assume. I exchange a quick glance with McCall. Both of us are still frozen in place and unsure of what to do.

"*Go, go, go!*" Cole shouts.

We try not to trip over one another as we run inside through the glass doors and leave a trail of sand behind us. Cole darts inside and tosses me a towel he had thrown over his shoulder.

I catch it, although I am caught off guard. "Thanks for being our *knight in shining armor*," I tease.

He flashes a shiny smile that fits his new persona. "Well, of course. *Doesn't every story need one?*"

Malik walks up to the three of us. He's fresh out of the shower with wet hair, no shirt, plaid pajama pants, and a puzzled expression on his face. "Why are y'all running in like a bunch of hooligans? What did I miss?"

"A possum. Where were you when we needed some help?" McCall retorts.

"Hey now! I had to beat the hot water rush," Malik revokes.

"Like you didn't get the hot water this morning. Twice in one day," she points out.

He shrugs, unbothered. "There's nothing wrong with being clean."

Cole and I share a look between their bickering. It's typical between siblings, but I don't know whether to laugh or ignore them altogether.

McCall turns to me. "I'm going to get in the shower and pray that there's hot water left."

I nod, noticing the small circle of sand around me. "I'll be upstairs soon. I'm going to clean up this sand before Aunt Sheryl sees the mess we've brought inside."

"I'll help." Cole nudges my arm, grinning. "We survived our second day."

MONDAY

5 Days Until the Wedding

MONDAY *playlist*

- All Day All Night ——————— Moon Taxi
- My Girl ——————— The Temptations
- 1 step forward, 3 steps back —— Olivia Rodrigo
- Catalonia ——————— Vance Joy
- Convertible in the Rain ——— Brynn Cartelli
- Play Pretend ——————— Alex Sampson
- Sh-Boom ——————— The Chords
- Fearless (*Taylor's Version*) ——— Taylor Swift
- Bahamas ——————— HARBOUR
- Coast ——— Hailee Steinfeld, Anderson .Paak
- Surfin' U.S.A. ——————— The Beach Boys
- Runaway Kids ——————— HARBOUR
- Sunshine ——————— OneRepublic
- Gimme! Gimme! Gimme! (A Man After Midnight) ——————— ABBA
- Lavender Haze ——————— Taylor Swift
- Taylor Swift ——————— Matt Cooper
- Shut Up and Dance —— WALK THE MOON
- invisible string ——————— Taylor Swift
- Really Wanna Dance With You —— New Rules
- Head Over Heels ——————— Tears For Fears
- Enchanted ——————— Taylor Swift

Chapter 13

TO SHARE OR NOT TO SHARE

While shopping yesterday, McCall and I passed a cute diner that seemed to be a local favorite, so we decided to drag the boys here for breakfast this morning.

The aesthetic of the Sunny Side Diner is complete with checkered floors, retro seating, waitresses in poodle skirts, and a working jukebox. It feels as though we've been frozen in time—*way before our time.*

"I'm so relieved to not be on breakfast duty this morning," McCall exclaims, taking a bite of her omelet.

"Mm-hmm," Malik agrees, shoving a fork full of pancakes into his mouth.

The food truly is *delicious.* Even though yesterday's French toast was amazing, I'm secretly glad we don't have to deal with the pesky smoke alarm.

From the rules we've been told at Hollow Oak, the food competitions will alternate meals and competitors each day. Today, two lucky or not-so-lucky people will be in charge of lunch. Aunt Sheryl noted that we could '*turn into hunters and gatherers*' to find food, but finding this vintage diner playing *My Girl by The Temptations* is more my style.

Based on the way Cole is singing into his fork, I'm guessing it's more his style as well.

"Say cheese!" McCall holds her phone on the other side of the booth, pointing the camera at Cole and me.

I lean closer to him, my head almost touching his shoulder. Cole also scoots closer, causing my head to now fully rest on his shoulder. Malik is chuckling from across the table, and I can only imagine what face Cole is making. I gently elbow him as I smile.

"Aw, that one's cute," McCall expresses as I hear the click of the camera.

"Do y'all have plans for today?" Malik asks.

Cole shrugs, looking confused and out of the loop. "Not that I know of."

"I was thinking we could go for a joy ride."

"Whoa, whoa," McCall stops him with one hand raised in the air. "A joy ride in what? *Dad's car?*"

Malik nods like it's no big deal. Simultaneously, his sister's expression says otherwise. "Yes. Dad's car," he responds.

"Have you asked him?"

"No, not yet. I was seeing if anyone had plans *first*. If y'all are up for it, *then* I'll talk him into it."

"I don't think he'll agree, but *if* you can convince him, I'm in," I say between bites of my toast. "Good luck."

"Why wouldn't you be able to take the car?" Cole begins to question. "Wait! Is your dad's car the vintage Bel Air?"

"The one and only." Malik draws in a sharp breath. "It's practically his third child."

"No, I'm more like his third child, and you're his second," McCall corrects. "That car is his first child—his big baby."

Questionably, Cole gives a look to Malik. "And you think you can talk him into letting *us* take it?"

"Oh yeah, I can talk my dad into *anything*. He's very easy to persuade."

McCall shakes her head. "Eh, that's debatable. His persuasiveness depends on what side of the bed he woke up on, so I guess only time will tell."

In Malik's search to find Uncle Malcolm, he had Cole accompany him. We've only been here a short time, and I'm glad to see that the boys are already bonding.

McCall and I relax on our beds, talking as we scroll on our phones. The signal here has proved to be spotty, and my phone consistently crashes at times, so

I'm shocked to see that it's working so well at the moment.

My phone dings with a text from McCall. I involuntarily grin when the photo she took this morning appears on the screen. In the photo, my smile is even wider than I remember. Cole is captured mid-laugh with squinted eyes and his mouth slightly open.

The two of us look happy in the photo. In fact, we look *more than happy.* In a way, we look like we're *more than friends.*

Since I'm already browsing social media, I have an idea. *To share or not to share?* What could it hurt?

I add a simple black-and-white filter to the photo and add it to my page. It's been nearly a minute since I shared, and I see that multiple people have already 'liked' it. My breath feels caught when I see who sits at the top of the list.

Jesse.

I didn't post it to make him jealous, although I have to admit that the thought of him seeing it feels good in its own selfish way. Knowing that he's seen me happy —not with him—is the sweetest revenge.

During our run-in at Wonderland Books, I told him that I had plans to bring someone else. My lie shortly became the truth when I spotted Cole outside that day. All weekend, Jesse's known that he had a replacement. He just didn't know who it was.

Of all people… *Cole.* The two of them have had issues with one another in the past. Or at least… Jesse has had an issue with Cole.

A notification pops up at the top of my screen: **JESSE IS TYPING.**

Without another thought, I go to his profile and hit **BLOCK THIS USER** before his message can send. Whatever it is or whatever it was going to be—I don't care to know.

I get out of bed, slide open the dresser drawer, and set my phone inside the empty compartment. *Out of sight, out of mind,* I think as I lock it away.

With the thought of my ex trying to contact me, I know exactly what I need—way more fresh air than this bedroom is currently offering. I let McCall know that I'll be back shortly and head outside.

As I go on a solo walk by the water, I let the memories of my past consume me.

Six and a half months ago, I went to a New Year's Eve party with Jesse. It was hosted by a friend of his, the star pitcher of our school's baseball team. Even though I went to school with the majority of the people there, they weren't exactly my group of friends. Past the point of recognizing them from the back row of my English class, I certainly couldn't hold a conversation with any of them.

Unlike me, Jesse seemed to know *everyone* at this party exceptionally well. He was practically friends with all of them—the people who were the well-known party-goers and even the ones who had passed out on the couch by 10:30.

All night, I awkwardly stood beside Jesse and followed behind him as he made his rounds. He didn't introduce me to anyone, and the other guys never acknowledged me. Most of them were his jock friends, meaning I was one in a handful of females. Many of the other girls looked like me in the way that they were following in their boyfriends' footsteps. When I did my best to talk to a few, Jesse's arm would wrap around my shoulder and tug me closer. It was as if he was making sure I was still there and focused on *him*. Eventually, I desperately needed a break from the fake smile, so I left his side for a few minutes.

I walked into the kitchen and spotted an unopened case of root beer. Helping myself, I pulled out a can, opened it with a *pop,* and leaned against the kitchen counter as I took a sip. It was then that I saw a familiar face walk through the front door—Cole.

He walked up to me and asked, "Where'd you get that?" He gently tapped the soda in my hand.

I motioned to the box that was shoved under the table. With Cole and I, there was rarely a need to exchange hellos. Since we saw each other daily, it felt weird to have any sort of formal greeting between us.

"Great. Thanks. I was worried someone spiked the punch."

I chuckled. In certain situations, it's almost like Cole and I have the same mind.

Amidst both of us laughing, Jesse came into my peripheral view. As he talked, his voice sounded both exhausted and agitated. "Finley! I was wondering where you ran off to." I watched as his gaze shifted to my left. A darker look took over his eyes. "Or *whom* you ran off to." He nearly scoffed.

"Hey, Jesse," Cole replied, civil and cheerful as always.

"What are you doing here?" Jesse questioned him as he draped his arm around me and pulled me close. I felt like nothing more than a trophy that he was trying to show off.

"Just stopped by to see Ross and the guys," Cole responded.

"Right," Jesse said, his tone stiff. "You ready, Finley?"

I looked at the time—it was only 11:20 PM... *at a New Year's Eve party.* "Um... sure? You don't want to stay until midnight?" I truly didn't want to come in the first place, but what difference would another forty minutes make?

Jesse narrowed his eyes toward Cole. "Nah, I'm a little over this party now. We can go get ice cream."

By leaving early, we'd be missing the fireworks, but I feared there would otherwise be *someone's temper* exploding in this kitchen if we didn't get out soon. With his arm still draped around me, Jesse and I walked toward the front door. I turned around and mouthed the most apologetic "I'm sorry," I could to Cole.

He shrugged with one shoulder and mouthed, "No worries."

After speeding off, Jesse was the first to speak up. "So, you deserted me to run off to Cole?"

I couldn't hide the bewilderment marked on my face. "*Excuse me?*"

"I mean you just left me, and then I found you with *him* of all people. What am I supposed to make of that?"

"Nothing." I shrug. "You weren't even talking to me, so I went to get a drink. Then he walked in. What's so wrong with that?" The fury had quickly risen in my chest.

"It's just *always* him!" Jesse threw a hand up in the air before letting it drop *hard* onto the steering wheel. He had never been physically abusive, but I still flinched like his hand was coming for me right that second. "I mean, seriously!" he continued. "He's always texting you, he's always at your house, and now tonight you two were flirting in front of my friends! Cole is *always* in the picture!"

"Flirting? And what *picture?*" I'm shouting now. I don't know if Jesse started yelling first, but both of our voices are amplified. "Cole is always around because he's my *neighbor*. He texted me *one* night while we were at the drive-in because I continuously missed Game Nights! I've known him since we were babies. Do you *seriously* expect me to just act like he doesn't exist?"

"Yes, actually! If you were in my shoes, that's what you would want. You're not with *him*, you're with *me!*"

My mouth had dropped. Somehow, I found the words amongst the built-up anger in me to start talking again. "You have to be joking right now, Jesse! You act like I'm cheating on you after I have two minutes of an innocent conversation with him! He's my friend and—"

"I'm not having this conversation right now." His breathing was deep as he threw his head against the headrest.

"What conversation? The one you started when we left the party because of your self-absorbed insecurity?" I cross my arms, angling my body in the opposite direction of his.

I told him to bring me home. *Screw the ice cream.*

I didn't ring in the new year with Jesse or a bunch of random people whom I pass in the school hallways.

From the moment I walked through the front door, I repeatedly dodged my mom's questions about why I was home earlier than expected. I knew she'd be on the phone with Mrs. Clara, and the last thing I needed was for Cole to know that I spent an entire car ride home in a fight with my boyfriend over him—*about* him. He didn't do anything wrong that night, and he hasn't done anything wrong in the past. There was no need for him to be worried about something that was… *nothing.*

There was no need for me to be worried either.

I focused on what mattered instead: my family. As we started the countdown to midnight, Ryder bounced around excitedly, ecstatic to be staying up way past his bedtime. When the clock struck twelve, my dad set off confetti poppers, I tossed Saylor into the air, my mom cheered, and Wren secretly chuckled at our madness, even though she acted too mature to enjoy it. *I started this year with my family—where I should've been all along.* When I'm not with them, I still want to be with people who *feel* like family.

The people who… love you for who you are, accept you with all of your flaws, can laugh with you over your weird quirks, and provide solid ground on your rough days.

I think it was that night when it truly clicked for the first time that Jesse isn't one of those people.

Chapter 14

JOY RIDE

Persuading Uncle Malcolm took some time, but he's allowed us to use the car—with stipulations. *Lots of them.*

The car must arrive back at Hollow Oak in pristine condition—just the way we took it with a full tank of gas, a shiny exterior, and a vacuumed interior. Malik is the only one allowed to drive—without speeding, of course. We are clearly not allowed to do anything reckless like burnouts, and we can't park near other cars for fear of someone else scratching the paint. With the list of rules to follow, I'm beginning to wonder if the boys signed a contract.

The 1957 Chevy Bel Air with a pale yellow tint sits flawlessly in the driveway with the top down. Typically, Uncle Malcolm only drives it around their hometown and to vintage car shows. He's made an exception this week, allowing Sierra and Dalton to use it as their grand wedding exit. Aunt Sheryl seems ecstatic that they're able to use it. '*Imagine the pictures!*' I heard her gushing to my mom yesterday.

Cole opens the passenger door, leans the front seat forward, and motions for me to sit in the back. "Ladies first," he says with a grin.

I smile as I climb in, but it quickly fades. With New Year's Eve fresh on my mind, I'm brought back to that night. As we were leaving the party, I opened my own car door, which was typical, while Jesse slammed his shut.

Once I slide across the leather seat, Cole scoots in beside me. Malik and McCall are climbing into the front seat as Uncle Malcolm shouts from the porch, "Be careful, kids! Don't forget my rules on your joy ride!"

We stay within the city limits of Sunrise Beach. Driving down the now familiar roads, we pass the Sunny Side Diner, then the small boutique where I tried on those funky sunglasses. Lastly, we pass the restaurant where the entire wedding crew ate dinner on our first night here. I glance at the parking lot where Cole let me practice holding his hand as I giggled like a little schoolgirl.

I've only been in this town for two days, and I already notice myself wishing I could stay longer. As I'm soaking in the beach view, I wonder if the locals ever get tired of watching the waves roll onto the sand.

Personally, I don't think this view could ever grow old. I love Whitefield, but there's something about Sunrise Beach that feels like a breath of fresh air. It's a feeling like anyone can come here and turn the page to a new beginning. Maybe it's just a tourist trap, but I don't mind being momentarily stuck in this cage. On our ride back through the main strip, I focus on the shops and try to make out each store's name. I notice that I've yet to see a bookstore anywhere in sight. One would certainly complete the small-town trifecta.

Cole scoots as close as his seat belt will allow, leaning in until his shoulder bumps into mine. "Whatcha thinking about?"

As I'm about to spurt out my default response of *Nothing*, I catch myself. "Honestly? I'm daydreaming about what it would be like to live here one day."

"Really?" he questions. His voice is loud, and his brown hair is blowing from the wind.

"You never know," I nonchalantly say. "From what I've seen, this simple town has everything... except a bookstore. Maybe I could open one."

Cole smiles. "Oh, yeah? I didn't realize you were the business type."

"I'm not." I chuckle, watching as the town passes in a blur. "But it would be a dream to own a bookstore in a place like this."

"Well..." he begins. "Lucky for you, I may know a guy with a business degree in a few years."

I turn to face him. "Who? *You?*"

"Yeah, I've decided to major in Business and Marketing."

I feel a pang of guilt for not knowing this. I guess my time spent with Jesse put a minor gap between Cole and me. We still talked but not to the extent of our younger days. At one point in our lives, we knew everything about one another, even our most embarrassing moments. And here we are now… with a lot of catching up to do. I guess it's a good thing we're staying under the same roof for a week.

Still, I smile at him. *For* him. "No way! That seems very fitting for you."

"You think?"

I begin to chuckle at the irony. "When we were on our way to Sunrise Beach, I thought you'd make a wonderful entrepreneur. You kept talking about selling the crap out of—" I stop, realizing I almost said '*our relationship*' while McCall and Malik are directly in front of us, possibly hearing everything we say since we're trying to talk over the wind.

He nods, understanding without me actually saying the words. "I guess I picked the right major then."

"Looks like you did."

"I can picture it right there," Cole exclaims, quickly pointing out my side of the car.

"Hmm?"

"That building right there. The white one." He points again. "That could be your bookstore one day. *Brooks' Books.*"

I smile, not only at his clever use of my last name for a storefront but also at the thought itself. I repeat it quietly, "*Brooks' Books*—I love it! I'll just have to find a *really* good business partner." I nudge him with my elbow. "Wanna make another pact?"

111

Unless I'm mistaken, I think I spot Cole shyly laughing before he glances in the other direction.

The four of us have agreed to check out a hidden gem in the next town over, and Malik turns down a side street that is unfamiliar to me.

McCall's hair is braided straight back into a short ponytail while mine is windblown and severely tangled. I silently curse myself for being so headstrong over my hair being down since my breakup with Jesse.

Blissfully, more minutes pass. The drive is peaceful... *until it's not.* The car now feels wobbly and unstable beneath us.

"What the...?" Malik questions from behind the wheel.

With the car slightly rocking, I accidentally bump into Cole. He leans forward, getting closer to the front seats as he says, "I think we need to pull over."

Malik does so, finding a spot to pull off.

We all get out to inspect the car. The driver's side seems perfectly fine. The door is still so clean I can practically see my reflection.

"Guys..." Cole cautions from beside the passenger door. "I think you're going to want to see this." He grimaces. "Actually, you might *not* want to see it."

Malik is quickly at his side. "No, no, *no.*" His panicked words are barely above a whisper. "I figured this was the problem, but I definitely didn't want to *believe* it."

McCall and I walk over, simultaneously spotting the issue. I gasp, placing a hand over my mouth. McCall sighs, turning to face Malik. "You better believe it—and we better fix it before Dad finds out."

The back tire is extremely *flat.* Unluckily for us, it's not the kind of 'flat' where we can just drive away and refill it with air. It's the kind of 'flat' that resembles a deflated beach ball. We're stranded in the middle of nowhere with a long screw sticking out of the tire.

To put it lightly... *we're actually screwed.*

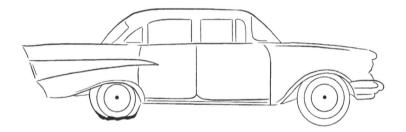

Chapter 15

ONE HORSE TOWN

Cole tries to reassure Malik. "Let's see if there's a spare, and I can change it. This should be an easy fix."

Almost immediately, Malik seems to lose his only sense of hope when they open the trunk to find nothing but an empty space.

"No luck?" McCall questions.

"Nope, there's no spare."

Malik is now pacing laps around the car as his words spit out frantically. "My dad is going to kill me."

McCall mutters, "Aunt Sheryl will probably kill us before Dad even gets a chance. I don't want to be a part of the debacle that messes up Sierra's wedding plans. This car is her request for *something borrowed.*"

"Now what?" Malik exasperates. "How is she going to borrow a stranded car?"

I quietly mention, "It's better that this happened to us now versus them on their wedding night, right?" I lightly shrug, trying to make this moment a little less tense.

"She does have a point," Cole agrees.

From the outside looking in, Malik appears to be your stereotypical jock who runs for fun and drinks protein smoothies. Although now, as we're stranded on the side of the road… it's apparent how dramatic he truly is. He asks, "Which do you like better—lilies or carnations? We'll need to plan my future funeral accordingly."

On the verge of laughter, Cole pats Malik on the back. "Dude, it's seriously okay. Flat tires happen all the time. I just changed a flat a few weeks ago on my car."

I lightly chuckle. "You mean, your minivan?"

"Wait," Malik says, momentarily pausing his funeral planning. "That's your minivan?"

"Well, it's technically not *mine*," Cole responds. "It's my mom's, but I also drive it."

"They share the van," I clarify.

Malik grins. "So you *do* drive a minivan!"

"Uhh… yeah?" Cole questions. "Do you have something against them?"

"Not at all. It's just not what I pictured you driving."

Cole exclaims, "Can we discuss the tire that you were having heart palpitations over? This conversation took a weird turn."

"I'd much rather focus on your *Mom Mobile* than my impending murder," Malik says.

"I'm guessing now is a bad time to say I have to pee?" I look around at our bare surroundings. "We're kind of stranded."

"Fin, we're *very* stranded," Cole remarks.

"Should we call Dad?" McCall suggests.

"Absolutely not!" Malik protests. "He cannot know about this. My phone's not even working out here. There's hardly any service as it is in this town, nonetheless wherever we are now."

Cole asks, "How far back was any sort of civilization?" He and I were in such deep conversation during the drive, we hardly paid attention to where we were.

"Past the long stretch of asphalt?" Malik winces. "At least three miles. We passed an old gas station a while back."

Cole turns to me. "You up for a walk? We could go back to call for a ride."

I glance down at my thin flip-flops, but I don't have much of a choice.

"Should we stay here?" McCall asks her brother.

"That's probably our best bet. I think I'd face a double death penalty if Dad finds out that I left the car stranded on the side of the road as well."

"Very valid point," I agree.

"Best-case scenario," Cole begins, "We quickly find civilization, get a new tire, and your dad never finds out." There's really no telling how long Cole and I could be gone or how long McCall and Malik will be standing watch on this deserted road.

"What about the worst-case scenario?" McCall warily questions.

Malik huffs. "We don't need any more negativity added to this situation." *Says the guy who has spent the past ten minutes planning his funeral.*

"It's a reasonable question," I point out. "What if someone drives by and y'all are able to get help before we do?" They all nod, seeming to agree with me. "If nothing else, we'll try to meet up at the Old Lavender House at five. Meeting at Hollow Oak may be a little too risky if Uncle Malcolm sees us without the car. If the other group isn't there yet..." My words trail off. "Well, let's just hope for the best."

"Just in case," Cole starts, "Let me give you my phone number. Fin doesn't have hers, so call me if anything happens."

"*If* we get a signal," Malik points out.

After a moment of sharing phone numbers and saying our short-term goodbyes, Cole outstretches his hand to me. I take it as we walk together, heading in the direction we just came from. Hopefully, the old gas station is closer than we think.

A few minutes have passed, and his hand being clasped in mine has yet to change. "I think we can let go now," I mention.

"Hmm?"

Wordlessly, I lift our intertwined hands. McCall and Malik are far behind now, surely not paying us any attention.

"*Oh*, right," he says, dropping my hand.

I smile. "We're getting a lot better at this fake dating scene."

"I can almost believe it myself."

The scary thing is… I sort of agree. I can see this relationship being real. Although rules are rules, and we have an entire crumpled-up receipt full of them. Within those rules… we already have a prewritten ending.

We've walked for what feels like hours. If not for the incessant pounding of flip-flops against my feet, it wouldn't be so bad. Although I wasn't intending on walking a 5K, this makes me question my taste in shoes.

Despite the annoying shoes, positive things are on the horizon. Cole and I are approaching our first sign of life in miles—a small building off in the distance.

As we get closer, I notice it's the gas station we've been holding out hope for. There are only two pumps, one of which has a piece of paper with the words '*OUT OF ORDER*' written in scraggly handwriting. There's a single car parked on the side of the building.

I turn to Cole. "I guess this is our only option."

He nods, wide-eyed.

Typically, this isn't a building I'd enter for fear of being kidnapped. Yet now, with a desperate need for a bathroom break and knowing that my cousins are stranded, I push open the scratched glass door. The bell rings over my head, slightly startling me. At first, there's not a single soul in sight. *So much for civilization.*

Cole takes the lead, walking us down the aisle of candy bars. As we round the corner, the checkout counter comes into view. We notice that there's no one behind the counter but soon spot an employee through an office door. "Excuse me," Cole exclaims.

The red-headed girl doesn't say anything. She's staring down at the phone in her hands as if it'll disappear into thin air if she looks away.

"Hi!" I try.

Still... *nothing.*

At this point, we're standing right in front of the register, and she's yet to even glance in our direction. I notice her white earbuds. I point this out to Cole by tapping my ear.

He waves his hand, attempting—and once again, failing—to get her attention. "Do you have a phone we could borrow?" he yells. The entire walk here, Cole kept checking for a signal on his phone. Eventually, his battery died. It's no use if McCall or Malik tries to call us now.

"Can we borrow a phone?" I loudly question.

Still not breaking eye contact with her screen, she finally responds. "Gas only, no diesel. Pump two is broken."

I'd like to consider myself a patient person, but I'm silently resisting the urge to take the phone out of her hand myself and find the number of a tow truck.

Cole must sense my patience thinning, or maybe his is as well because he continues even louder than before. "A *phone!* Can we use a phone?"

She shakes her head. "No ice cream cones. Only soda and candy."

Oh. My. Word. If we were robbing this chick, we could've scoured every square foot of this place by now. Finally, I've had enough. My feet hurt, my bladder is about to explode, and this run-down gas station was our best bet at finding help. Losing all composure, I grab a king-sized candy bar from the shelf beside me and throw it in her direction. It makes it through the doorway and lands at her feet. Clearly offended, her head shoots up.

She removes one of her earbuds. "*What.*" She doesn't phrase it as a question.

"We need a phone," I say flatly. "Our friends are currently in the middle of this one-horse town, and we need a way to contact someone. Now, if you could help us and—"

"*Finley*," Cole mutters under his breath. Nice as ever, he smiles at the girl.

I clear my throat and continue, this time with a more polite tone and a forced smile. "Please, if we could borrow the gas station's phone for just a second, or if you can help us for one moment to find the number of a tow truck, that'd be great."

"I know a guy," she declares. "Follow me." She rises from her seat and walks further back into the store. Slightly worried, I glance at Cole. He shrugs, wordlessly saying, *What else are we supposed to do?* He steps in front of me, trailing the girl. We walk down a short hallway, and my flip-flops echo even more in the enclosed space. At the end of the hallway sits a baby blue rotary phone.

She lifts her finger, pointing to the corkboard beside it. "His name is Barry. Or maybe it's Gary? I can't remember, but it's on the board somewhere. Once you find it and call him, please feel free to sit *outside*." With that, she places the earbud back into her ear and walks off.

"So we're looking for a Barry," I exclaim.

"Or a Gary," Cole says, a smile in his tone.

I chuckle. "Time for you to figure it out, Sherlock. I'm going to the bathroom."

Once I return and take a look at the board, it truly looks worthy of a Sherlock Holmes case. Every inch of the corkboard is filled with papers ranging from take-out menus, post-it notes, thumbtacks, and lots of illegible handwriting. There is way too much useless information in this dark hallway. I can only hope that something useful is mixed in with the chaos.

Cole removes a piece of paper from the board and passes it to me. "Do you think this could be him? He's an *-erry*." Although it's not Barry *or* Gary—it's Terry.

Grinning, I say, "It's worth a shot."

The girl seemed annoyed by us after we interrupted her, so we took her not-so-subtle offer to wait outside. We're sitting on the curb, leaning back against the broken gas pump.

After we spend a few minutes joking about the *world's best employee*, Cole begins. "I think I figured you out."

"Figured *me* out? What is there to figure out? I'm an open book."

He continues with a playful tone in his voice. "Yeah, a mystery book. You're just full of plot twists, aren't you?"

"What do you mean?" I ask, genuinely intrigued.

"You're so predictable, yet you're so full of surprises. Take the gas station girl for example. I knew you were bound to do something to get her to listen, but I definitely wasn't expecting you to throw a candy bar at her."

"She wasn't paying any attention to us!" I chuckle.

"That's what I mean though," Cole says with a smile. "You're going to make something happen. When Jesse asked for his spot back as a date, you told him you already had one. You clearly didn't at the time, but sure enough…."

"…Here we are now."

"But while we're on this topic," he jokes, "I think you've secretly been planning this your whole life."

"*Pssh,*" I laugh. "Don't flatter yourself, Baxter. But I need you to elaborate on that one."

"You tried to kiss me in Kindergarten."

"I did not!" I laugh. "I have no memory of that *whatsoever.*"

"Oh, I remember it vividly! We were in the treehouse."

I slowly nod for him to continue. Growing up, we were always in the treehouse. *That* part is believable. The kiss... *not so much.*

He chuckles. "I just remember you coming toward me, lips puckered. Obviously, I moved out of the way."

"You're such a liar." I grin, playfully pushing him away.

"I'm definitely not a liar. You just have an awful memory."

"If your memory is so good, then why did I try to kiss you?" I press.

"We were like five, how would I know? I have no clue what your motive was, only that you must've been daydreaming about me."

"Your story has to be backward. Maybe *you* were dreaming of *me* back then."

"Oh, all the time," he jokes. *At least I think he's joking.*

A vehicle pulls into the gas station. With our one ounce of good luck, it has *Terry's Tow Truck & Co.* printed on the side.

"At last," I say with a relieved sigh.

We raise from our spot on the curb, desperately meeting the driver at his door as he's stepping out.

"Hey," Cole speaks up first. "Are you Terry?"

With a head of gray, balding hair, the driver nods. "The one and only! What's our issue here folks? I'm not exactly seeing a car that's in need of a tow."

"Well," I begin, grimacing as I picture my abandoned cousins on the side of the road. "About that...."

Chapter 16

NO FULL TRUTHS

As it turns out, Terry, of *Terry's Tow Truck & Co.*, is a *talker*. He reunited us with McCall, Malik, and the 1950s convertible. He loaded it up, brought us to a tire shop, and sat with us until the new tire was put on… but he didn't do any of this without stories—*lots of them*. This man needs an outlet to share and converse with others who are not teenagers with no escape plan.

He talked the most about his four-year-old granddaughter, Betty. She performed in her first dance recital last month, and according to Terry, she ran off stage while yelling that she had to go potty. Her fellow four-year-old dancers looked beyond confused by this, and some even tried to follow her off the stage. Terry, *over a month later*, still finds this story absolutely hilarious. He spent the entire ride to the car explaining this to Cole and me… and then continued to re-explain the story to McCall and Malik on our way to the tire shop. As he told the mediocre story, he snorted in laughter and was *literally* slapping his knee. I think we all laughed more at *him* than at his story.

Once the tire is replaced, Malik is back in full panic mode. "What are we going to tell him?" he asks.

I shrug, easily finding a cover story. "Nothing. Our joy ride just took longer than expected. After all, we still have to find a car wash with vacuums. We can blame it on that."

"And *lie* to my dad?"

McCall is looking just as—*if not more*—stressed than her brother. "I'm such an awful liar."

"We wouldn't *necessarily* be lying," I say. "It really did take longer than expected. We just won't be telling the full truth."

Cole nods. "I think it's worth a shot. The tire looks the exact same to me."

It's not a shock to see that he is willing to go along with the plan. We're far from being pathological liars, but we have been telling our fair share of white lies —or at least, *not telling the full truth*—to everyone since we arrived. In their eyes, we are a happy couple.

I face Cole as I continue. "Exactly. We need to *sell it.*"

"Fine," McCall says with a sigh. "I'm in, but I can *not* do any of the talking."

At the Hollow Oak Beach House, we manage to convince Uncle Malcolm that everything went off without a *hitch*. Obviously, we didn't mention the fact that we had to *hitch a ride* from a tow truck. We didn't let McCall do any of the talking, and no one mentioned the number of stipulations we failed to follow.

Luckily for us, we avoid answering too many questions since we couldn't hear over the smoke alarm, and Uncle Malcolm was busy in his search for a ladder. Blaire and Peyton are making cookies. They're baking to perfection, without a trace of anything burning in the air, and the smoke detector is still relentless.

"Eddie!" Aunt Sheryl calls out as she swats at it with a hand towel. "Do you have the number of the venue owner?" *Beep, beeeep!*

"What?" he shouts from the living room couch.

"Do you have the number?"

"I can't hear you over all this beeping!"

Aunt Sheryl storms into the living room, annoyed beyond measure. "Maybe you could hear me if you got off the couch!"

"Sorry, dear," he says, almost monotone.

Beep, beep, beep, and just when I think it's over —*BEEEEP!*

"Now, will you call the venue owner? *They will hear it from me* if they don't have someone over to fix this by tomorrow morning!"

"Sure thing, dear." Eddie takes his phone and walks outside. For the sake of the venue owner not getting the full extent of Aunt Sheryl's wrath, I sure hope he gets in contact with them soon.

On Sunday, as McCall was burning batch after batch of French toast, the beeping seemed warranted. But ever since then, it's gone off any time the stovetop is turned on or the oven door is open. For crying out loud, it even went off once when Malik was using the blender to make his protein smoothie. The smoke alarm has truly gone *haywire*.

We've tried everything to stop the perpetual beeping the past couple of days. Due to the high ceilings, no one is able to reach it without a ladder. Even after Aunt Kira stuck a broomstick in the air and pressed the button, it didn't help whatsoever. Nearly every hand towel at Hollow Oak has been waved in the air in an attempt to stop the high-pitched screeching.

With Saylor and Juniper running laps around one another and the smoke detector that seems to grow louder by the second, it's pure chaos inside. I find myself missing the peace Cole and I had while sitting outside the gas station. It was relaxing, even though we were sitting on concrete and he was making up a story about me trying to kiss him in Kindergarten. Although, maybe it *was* true and I had just forgotten. I've never liked Cole in any way other than as a friend, but I've dreamt of happily ever afters for as long as I can remember. Maybe my younger self thought he would be my Prince Charming.

Now craving the beach view, I walk outside. I find myself going from one extreme to the next.

"Finley, perfect!" Sierra calls from the sand. "Come help us out. We could use someone else on our team!"

If I've learned anything, it's that there's usually some form of competition going on at this house. Due to the tire situation earlier, we missed the lunch cook-off. I heard the house of the groom won, and Eddie isn't ecstatic about it.

A volleyball bounces over the net from one group of people to the next.

Cole grins, waving me over. "Come on, Fin!"

I'm shockingly now glad for my thin flip-flops. They're easy to slide off and toss to the side. I join the team consisting of Sierra, Cole, my dad, Ryder, Malik, and Matt. Eddie is surprisingly absent. Maybe he's still trying to get in touch with the venue owner.

Jacob—one of the groomsmen—serves, and the ball flies over the net in my direction. I dive for it but fall short by less than a foot. Luckily, Cole has me covered as he swoops in and hits it. With my knees in the sand, I watch as the ball floats up and my dad hits it hard onto the other team's side. It hits the ground with a *thud*.

"*Ayy!*" Cole cheers. "Go, Mr. River!" He turns to my dad, raising his hand.

My dad gives him a high-five, *surely* saying something cheesy about '*teamwork making the dream work*'.

Even though interactions between the two of them aren't rare by any means, it's nice to see them together like this. Truly, it's a little endearing to see Cole getting close to all of my family.

I think back to Saturday when we first arrived at Hollow Oak. As a line of my family came trailing out the front door, it was almost weird and unnatural to see my extended family and Cole together in the same space— my two worlds colliding into one.

And yet currently, nothing feels more natural. It's like the fates and the stars all aligned to give me this week with my family… *and him*. Maybe he was supposed to come here all along. It just took some very questionable life choices for it to happen.

Chapter 17

MEET ME AT MIDNIGHT

The Hollow Oak Beach House (Bride): 3
The Old Lavender House (Groom): 1

According to Eddie, staying in the lead and ahead of the game is *crucial*... but I'm also *exhausted* by trying to do so.

While I attempt to read a little before bed, I feel myself beginning to doze off. I'm not even a chapter in, and I can hardly keep my eyes open. I tell McCall goodnight as I set my book on the bedside table and turn off the lamp.

My nighttime retainer is in my mouth, my hair has been braided post-shower, and I have a pimple patch over the blemish on my chin. I'm wishing the pimple away before it ends up in every wedding photo. My legs are freshly shaven and are feeling the utmost level of comfort with the silk sheets over me.

Just as I get situated in a comfortable position, a knock sounds at our door. Creaking as it opens ever so slightly, Malik's head peaks through the opening. *"Psst,"* he hisses. "Are y'all awake?"

I prop myself up on my elbows and respond, *"Barely."*

Cole's head pops in over Malik's as if they're in a 90s sitcom. "We're hungry."

"Right now?" McCall questions, sitting up in her bed. She sounds just as tired as I feel.

Quietly, the boys scurry into our room and close the door behind them. Malik flicks the overhead light on, and my eyes squint due to the drastic change in lighting.

"Ughhh," McCall groans. "Go make yourself something to eat."

Malik looks seriously offended at this idea. "And chance the smoke alarm waking everyone up at midnight? *No thank you!* I don't want to deal with an angry Aunt Sheryl in her hair rollers."

I chuckle at the mental image. "Then what's your solution? We don't have any food stored in our room."

"Sunny Side Diner?" Cole suggests. "We checked their website, and they're open until 2 AM."

Despite my heavy eyelids, I now notice the growl in my stomach. Thanks to the tire conflict, we missed lunch and ate an early dinner. Turning to McCall, I admit, "I could honestly go for a burger right now."

She throws her blanket to the side. "I'll get my shoes."

Discreetly—or at least as discreetly as possible—we file down the stairs and into the main area. Luckily for us, everyone else was also exhausted and called it an early night. No one was up talking or playing card games at the kitchen table like the past few nights. Cole grabs his car keys from his pocket. As they begin to rattle, we rush out the front door. The outside air is crisp, a kind of cool that only comes along with summer nights on the water.

"Nice!" Malik grins as he climbs in the back. "We get to ride in Cole's infamous minivan."

"Hey now!" Cole defends. "It's only infamous because you made fun of it. Cornelia is great."

"You named it?" I ask, buckling my seatbelt. "Named *her?*"

Bluntly, Cole laughs. "No, I'm just messing with y'all."

"Phew, I thought I was being replaced."

Malik sighs. "I can't believe I'm now stuck in the backseat with you two lovebirds up there."

I turn to face him as we pull out of the driveway. "You lost your driving privileges after today's fiasco. You better get used to the backseat of Cornelia."

"Ha!" McCall barks out a laugh beside him.

We pull into the parking lot and question whether they're still open. The website states that they're open until 2:00, but the Sunny Side Diner is just as deserted as the gas station from earlier today. Other than the four of us, there's a single waitress in red-rimmed glasses and a long poodle skirt. Very few sounds are coming from the kitchen.

The boys are in their own conversation, and as McCall is listening in, I yawn and feel myself beginning to drift off. We're seated next to the jukebox, so I get up to check it out with hopes that some music may bring me back to life. There's a catalog of songs, and nearly all of them are from the 20th century. I scroll through, recognizing Madonna, the Beach Boys, ABBA, Journey, and many other classics.

"Does anyone have any change?" I ask.

Cole stands and pulls a few quarters from his pocket. "Ooh, can I choose the first one?"

"Make it a good one."

"I gotcha covered." He inserts the change, presses a few buttons, and takes a few steps back on the checkered floor. The beginning beat of a Tears For Fears song is echoing around the small diner as he outstretches a hand to me. "Can I have this dance?"

"*Hmph*," I nearly laugh. "You want me to *dance?*"

"Well, I'd prefer that over you just staring at me."

"I cannot dance," I warn, shaking my head as I begrudgingly step forward and take his hand in mine. I can't help but notice the smile forming on my lips as we begin to awkwardly sway together. "This is ridiculous."

Cole grins. "Nah, this is *fun.*"

Still seated at the booth, McCall and Malik glance our way.

I can't believe the lengths we've gone to for a relationship that doesn't really exist, I think as we dance around in an uneven circle.

His hands are on the center of my back, and mine are draped over his shoulders. Moving over the checkered floor, it feels as if we're pieces in a game of chess where Cole and I serve as The King and Queen. The more we dance—*or do our best to dance*—the farther away we get from our table.

'*Something happens and I'm head over heels',* the lyrics sing.

"One way or another, you're always forcing me to listen to your music," I joke, thinking back to the days we would carpool to school and his music was blasting before I could even get in the passenger seat.

"I am not!" Cole deflects. "This is your music too."

"I hate to break it to you, but this is *not* Taylor Swift."

He smiles. "I don't think her prime has been in the era of jukeboxes."

"I guess not," I shrug with a smile.

Listening to the song, I let myself lean closer into Cole.

Even though this would not have been my first choice of song or artist… this moment does feel very Taylor Swift-*esque.* I'm sure she could put this feeling—

this emotion—into the perfect invisible string of lyricism.

One wispy strand of hair has fallen out of my braid and over my eye. As I push it back, I feel something on my face—my pimple patch. *How embarrassing!* Even though the patch is still on my chin and I'm wearing pajamas with bunny slippers, this still feels like one of the sweetest moments Cole and I have ever shared. Truly, it's one of the sweetest moments that I've shared with anyone. After all, we're slow dancing at midnight in an unoccupied diner that looks like it belongs in Stars Hollow. It's an enchanting sight.

My stomach flutters. Maybe it's the thought that all these moments with Cole will be ending soon... or maybe I'm just really starving.

TUESDAY
4 Days Until the Wedding

TUESDAY playlist

- Don't Kill My Vibe ———————— Sigrid
- i'm too pretty for this ———— Claire Rosinkranz
- Gaslighter ———————————— The Chicks
- The Great War ——————— Taylor Swift
- Riptide ————————————— Vance Joy
- New Religion ——————— The Haydaze
- Mess It Up ——————— Gracie Abrams
- We Didn't Start the Fire ——————— Billy Joel
- The Very First Night (*Taylor's Version*) (*From The Vault*) ———————————— Taylor Swift
- As It Was ——————————— Harry Styles
- The Idea of You ———— Grady, lovelytheband
- THE LITTLE THINGS ——— Kelsea Ballerini
- Dancing in the Moonlight ————— Toploader
- Loverboy ———————————————— A-Wall
- Snow On The Beach — Taylor Swift, Lana Del Rey

Chapter 18

HAVING
A BLAST

Mrs. Esther, Eddie's mother, sits at the front of the room at her own special table as she cranks the handle of an old-time bingo roller. The entirety of Hollow Oak, minus the small children, sits before her. A few guests from the Old Lavender house have joined in as well. Some people are on the couch with bingo sheets laid across their lap, some are seated at the island, and others, like Cole and myself, are on the floor. Even with the house's open floor plan, it easily gets crowded with so many people in one space.

"I-16!" Esther calls out. The rasp is prominent in her tone.

Everyone looks over their papers with bingo daubers at the ready. Cole turns to me, whispering, "What exactly are we trying to accomplish here? We're a few minutes in, and I'm still lost."

"A large picture frame," I whisper back. With his only response being a puzzled expression, I elaborate further. "It's basically a square all around your box." I use my finger to outline the area I'm talking about.

He uses his dauber to mark out I-16, and a blob of blue ink fills the space. "I always thought bingo was more simple than this—just a standard five in a row."

"O-72!" Esther shouts.

"Sometimes, yes," I respond. "When Esther is in charge? Never. She's a bingo fanatic but hates standard bingo with a passion."

He nods slowly, trying to focus. His focus is interrupted when his phone vibrates in his pocket. It barely makes any noise over the chatter of everyone in the room. He pulls it out, looking at the notification. "What a jerk," he exclaims.

"B-5!" Esther yells, then coughs.

"What's wrong?"

He shoots me a look like I might not *want* to know. "See for yourself."

As he passes the phone, it takes me a second to wrap my head around what's on his screen. There's a picture from yesterday that I didn't even realize was taken. It was during our peaceful ride in the convertible. I was looking out my side of the car, captured with a blur of blue skies and perfectly white sands behind me. There was a slight smile on my face, and I looked content... *happy*. In the picture, there's the location of Sunrise Beach and words that read, '*Having a blast*,' followed by the white heart emoji.

I smile as I see the moment that Cole perfectly captured. My smile drops when I see the reply on the picture. Or rather, when I see who sent it. Jesse's message reads as follows:

SO GLAD TO SEE THE TWO OF YOU ARE 'HAVING A BLAST'. CONGRATS ON BEING HER SECOND CHOICE. ALSO—TELL F HEY FOR ME? LOOKS LIKE SHE HAS ME BLOCKED ON EVERYTHING NOW. YOU DON'T HAPPEN TO KNOW WHO TALKED HER INTO THAT, DO YOU?? GO HAVE A BLAST, COLE.

I scoff with my mouth wide open. "Are you kidding me? What a passive-aggressive—"

"Bingo!" Peyton cheers, waving her winning sheet in the air with glee.

"I know." Cole nods, ignoring the bingo just as much as I do. "He's a little absurd."

"You're telling me. I don't know how I liked him for so long."

"Honestly?" Cole starts wearily. "I've never liked the guy, Fin. Even in elementary school, he would cheat during PE games."

"You should've warned me," I joke. "It seems like he's always been a cheater."

"At least you get a fresh start this week." He smiles and outstretches his hand to me.

At first, I think he's joking by the gesture. Even if he is, and even if it makes me look dumb, I take his hand. I find comfort in his steadiness and solid ground that I feel I have been lacking. Once again, I momentarily let myself believe the act.

Chapter 19

ALL IS FAIR IN LOVE & COMPETITION

After bingo, Sierra called all the bridesmaids over to discuss and finalize our beauty plans for the wedding. We agreed on simple hairstyles that we'll be styling ourselves. Caroline is in cosmetology school and has agreed to do everyone's makeup early that morning. Sierra confirmed our nail appointment for this Thursday, and we made the decision on our nail color—a shade of lavender so light that it's nearly white. As the big day gets closer, my excitement grows, and I know Sierra's excitement grows *tenfold*. She and Dalton get giddy just standing in the same room at the thought of what is to come. If plans could change, I think they would both walk down the aisle right this second.

In other news… we're now able to cook without hearing the ear-piercing screech of the smoke alarm! Eddie was able to get ahold of the venue owner, and they sent out a maintenance worker to fix it this morning.

Cooking in the sounds of family chatter and laughter rather than beeps has been a huge relief.

Eddie is itching for everyone to begin today's competitions since he claims the bridesmaids took too long with our beauty agenda. As he explains the rules to us in the sand, I feel a rush of comforting deja vu. It seems as though these games and the near chaos surrounding this week have become the usual ordeal.

Today, we'll be doing a series of challenges, most of which will tie into the wedding in one way or another. Each race or game will count as one point for the winning team. Eddie has a small chalkboard and a stick of chalk in hand to keep score.

Challenge #1: A classic relay race, but with a wedding twist. Instead of the typical baton, we are using a ring box. A gazebo sits off in the distance. We'll be racing there and back before passing the ring box to our teammate next in line.

My little brother, Ryder, will be racing first for our team. He is the real ring bearer, after all, so he's getting in some much-needed practice beforehand. We form a line behind him as the groom's team lines up to our left.

"On your mark," Eddie begins, "Get set... *go!*"

"Go, Ryder!" I cheer for him. Considering how short his eight-year-old legs are, he is doing great.

"Come on, little man!" Cole shouts with his hands cupping his mouth.

Ryder taps the gazebo with his free hand, turns around, and sprints back. It's almost unbelievable how fast he is going… until he isn't going fast at all. His legs can't seem to keep up with the rest of his body, and he topples forward, launching himself face-first into the sand. The ring box flies from his grasp.

"*Ouch*," Sierra grimaces. "It's okay, Ryder!"

He stands up groggily, wipes at the grains of sand that cover him, and reaches for the box. Eventually, he's up and jogging—*no longer sprinting*—back to us. Malik is up next and bolts toward the gazebo in an attempt to make up for the lost time. The second person from the groom's team is well in the lead and has already made it to the gazebo.

Unfortunately, they stayed in the lead round after round. No matter how fast we tried to run—and believe me, *we tried*—challenge number one ended up with a chalk tally for the groom's team. Ryder looks completely defeated.

I bend down, wiping more sand off his shirt. "It's okay, bud. We'll get 'em next time!"

Cole walks over and gives Ryder a high-five. "Good job, little dude! You had a lot of speed going down there."

"Yeah," he sadly agrees. "I didn't have speed coming back, though. I fell, and then I was super slow."

"Happens to the best of us. Let me tell you a quick story," Cole starts, bending down so he's at Ryder's level. "When we were younger, your sister and I always played tag. I was so fast that I was too hard for her to catch. There were quite a few days that Finley fell *much* worse than you did."

"Great story," I say in a monotone voice.

Cole continues, leaning in closer to Ryder and getting quiet. "But between you and me, there were also days when I fell too. Some days, she caught me." He looks up at me with a grin, and I can't help but smile myself.

Challenge #2: The Bouquet Toss. This is similar to a water balloon toss where you throw it to your partner, and you both take a step back until it drops. Only now, instead of water balloons, we're using cheap bouquets. The faux leaves practically fall off by the third toss, but we continue anyway. Thanks to Malik and Matt's catching abilities… the bride's team earns our first point of the afternoon.

Challenge #3: A wheelbarrow race. Honestly, there's not a single aspect of this challenge that can be related to a wedding… or the decor. I think Eddie just wanted to see someone fall on their face—and they do that *wonderfully*. Caroline and Blaire represent our team. The race ended with Eddie begrudgingly tallying a point for the groom's team, and Caroline being certain she sprained her knee. She sits off to the side in an Adirondack chair as she elevates her leg with ice. That makes two down from the bride's team.

Challenge #4: Tug of War. It's your typical game, only the lavender ribbon that marks the center of the rope is the same kind that will later be used for the wedding decorations. Aunt Sheryl has been toying with the ribbon all week, crafting centerpieces and tying huge bows for the backs of chairs. We split into our respectable teams, everyone grabbing ahold of the long rope and staking their feet into the ground.

With the force of everyone tugging, my feet slide in the sand. I'm brought back to Sunday night when Cole practically dragged me into the ocean.

If only I could pick up a few opponents from Dalton's side as Cole did to me. Instead, I just pull the rope harder and harder. My hands burn, but I don't give up just yet. Neither does the rest of my team.

The purple ribbon wavers, bouncing back from one side to the next. I keep my grip steady, Peyton and Caroline cheer from their seats, and Cole hugs the rope even closer to him. And yet… it's still not enough. In one swift motion, the ribbon flies over to the groom's side.

Eddie draws a sharp line on his chalkboard without saying a word as if he's proctoring a test and we all just received an *F*.

The Hollow Oak Beach House: 4

The Old Lavender House: 4

With the scoreboard now tied, there's only one challenge left for the time being.

Challenge #5: A three-legged race. We'll be using the same lavender ribbon to tie our legs together.

Each team is set to pick two people to represent them. The groom's team picks Ross and Bethany. Ross is a groomsman, and Bethany is his girlfriend who's waiting '*any day now*' for a proposal. I know this because Bethany is very loud and clear when expressing her thoughts at family meals. Ross truthfully looks a little frightened by her, but I can't say that I blame him.

Cole steps forward with his hand raised. "Finley and I will do it!"

I stand next to him, trying to hide my inner thoughts. The last time I even *attempted* a three-legged race was probably thirteen years ago at an Easter egg hunt.

"Perfect!" Sierra grins. "Finley and Cole, it is."

Aunt Sheryl ties the ribbon in a double knot around our legs. Cole and I stumble over to the starting line, and I realize that this will probably be *much* harder than I remember.

"Please don't make us fall," I whisper.

Eddie starts, "3... 2..."

"No promises," Cole responds.

"1!" Eddie shouts.

We take off. Running in the sand is hard enough on its own, so it's especially challenging when you're strapped to someone else. The same rules apply as prior races, so we're *hobbling* our way to the gazebo. With the wind whipping in my ears, I can barely make out a murmur of encouraging voices behind us.

We have our arms wrapped around one another's backs, doing our best to keep steady. We find a rhythm once we're halfway to our turning point. I step right, we step together. I step right, we step together.

"There we go!" I shout.

At this rate, we're so far in the lead that I can't even see Ross and Bethany in my peripheral vision. We tap the gazebo, racing back even faster than before. When we cross the finish line, Eddie's thrilled to make a chalk tally on *our* side of the board.

"Yay!" I cheer.

As well as we were able to coordinate in the actual race, the ribbon tied around our ankles doesn't work in our favor now. I jump up as Cole stands still. His weight keeps me down and sends me toppling over. He tries to catch me, but it just sends him falling with me.

We crash into the sand with intertwined arms, legs, and a tangle of purple ribbon. I squint, fearful of sand flinging into my eyes.

Cole laughs from overtop of me. When I open my eyes, his face is only inches away from mine. His arms are cradling the back of my neck and shoulders, holding me tight. We stay like this, frozen for only a moment, but it feels so much longer in my mind.

"Sorry," I breathe out, my words barely a whisper. I can't help but notice all the eyes lingering on us and the small whisper of chuckling voices.

Cole shrugs, smiling. "No worries, Babe. A little dirt never hurt, right?"

Malik bends down beside us, untying the ribbon that holds us together. "This is *sand*, Romeo."

Chapter 20

FUEL TO THE FIRE

Everyone is gathered outside as Eddie announces tonight's meal, chicken cooked to the choice of the lucky four chosen. "From the house of the groom," he says, reaching into one of the glass bowls, "Dylan and Natalie."

Dalton's parents step forward. Ecstatic, they high-five one another, and it's just as cheesy as you could imagine.

Aunt Sheryl reaches in and circles her hand around the second bowl, swirling the slips of paper.

Cole leans in close to me, whispering, "I feel bad for whoever is chosen."

"Now, from the bride's household… Finley and Jes—*Cole*," she says, correcting herself at the last second. "Finley and Cole will be representing the house of the bride."

Other than my expression dropping in utter shock, I stand frozen. I've been secretly hoping that my name would not be chosen in the lottery of who cooks a meal for the entire wedding party. It is rather the opposite—we're stuck with the hardest meal thus far, and with my cooking abilities, it's sure to turn out awful.

"The time starts now, and we'll see you all back here in a few hours for the judging!"

"And the feast," Mrs. Natalie happily notes. I'm sure she and Mr. Bray have been cooking together for decades.

Everyone disperses, branching off into different groups. I still don't think I've moved more than a mere inch. I'm so unsure of what I'm doing, I don't even know where to begin.

Cole turns to me. "This is going to be interesting."

The two of us slowly make our way into the kitchen and begin searching for any supplies and ingredients we think we'll need. We've cooked next to nothing since we've been here, so Cole and I are both opening and closing all the cabinets in an attempt to find anything helpful.

"Your mom went through a huge batch cooking phase last year, right?" I ask amidst my search for the aluminum foil. "Did she teach you anything? Do you even know the first thing about cooking?"

"Do I *look* like Paula Dean to you?"

I chuckle at his comment. "I'm serious! You didn't learn anything?"

"I honestly don't remember it." He bends down, looking under the sink for something. "I never actually *learned* when she tried to teach me. Normally I'd just make up an excuse. I'd usually end up at your house since *your* mom wasn't trying to force me to cook."

"*That's* why you were at my house so much last year?" I open even more cabinets, still looking for the dang aluminum foil. This kitchen seems to have an infinite number of cabinets, and I've yet to pick the correct one.

"One of the reasons," Cole says. "Sometimes, I told my mom I was going to help you with your Language homework."

"I'm great at Language!"

Cole grins the same mischievous grin he had when we were younger and doing something bound to get us both into trouble. "From my mom's perspective, you have *me* to thank for that… even though my Language grade was probably way worse than yours."

I shake my head, laughing. "I can't believe you lied about helping me with homework, and you just ended up just sitting on the couch, watching The Vampire Diaries instead."

He lifts a finger. "Hey! I *mostly* did it to get out of cooking."

"Well, now is not a great time for attempting our first big meal. The pressure is on." *Finally*, I find the aluminum foil.

Cole definitely does *not* look like Paula Dean. He *certainly* doesn't cook like her, either. Then again, neither do I. We have essentially been destined for failure as soon as our names were drawn from the bowl.

Neither of us has ever cooked chicken—or really *anything* above the skillset of grilled cheese, so we turn to the internet for help. With our luck, the first instructional video we click on shows a man speaking French—which we've never learned. The second video contains too many ingredients—which we either don't have on hand or can't find in the labyrinth of cabinetry. The third video we choose seems to be the most helpful so far. '*Mixing it Up with Margot*' possibly has more southern charm than Paula Dean and claims to make each dish with love as if she's cooking for her grandchildren.

We go back and forth between watching the video on Cole's phone and doing our best to replicate it. Granted, our '*best*' probably isn't all that good considering we don't know what we're doing, and we're trying to fast-forward through parts of the video. There's a slew of spices, cooking oils, and other ingredients lining the countertop. For everyone's sake, I hope it turns out fully cooked and doesn't give anyone food poisoning.

Mr. Dylan and Mrs. Natalie chose to make their chicken on the grill, and it seems to have worked up a crowd. Everyone from the Hollow Oak crew has dissipated to the back patio of the groom's house.

As I add the final blend of seasoning to the chicken, I ask Cole, "Have you heard anything else from Jesse today?" As much as it pains me, my brain can't seem to stop thinking about the message Cole received from him earlier.

"Nope, I didn't respond. I'm not sure if that will just add more fuel to his fire or what," he responds while picking up the ingredients we no longer need.

I scoff. "His fire is never-ending. Whether you added more fuel or not, I'm sure it'll keep burning for his own self-absorbed reasons."

"Have you heard anything from him?"

"No, I blocked him on everything."

"Understandable." Cole pauses for a moment, then lets out a low huff. "Fin, I hope you know that you deserve much better than him and the way he treated you."

"Thank you," I smile softly, unsure how else to respond. "And thank you for coming here with me, even if it has turned part of your summer break upside down. I know you didn't plan on partaking in a fake relationship, but it's really meant a lot to me."

"No, it's been great."

"For the longest time, I pictured Jesse on this trip. Then after our breakup, I knew I'd be here alone. Weirdly enough, when I told him I had a date, I felt the need to prove something to him. And I guess…" I pause, my words trailing off as I attempt to gather my thoughts.

"You guess...?" he questions, placing the pan in the oven and shutting the door.

"I proved something to myself instead. At the end of our relationship, I didn't really feel like *myself.* I felt more like the version that he wanted me to become. I've realized that I'm good by myself, but I'm also good with people who make me feel like *me.*" I glance at him with a not-so-sly smile.

"Yeah, I get that. It's only been a few days, but I think this trip has proved some things to me too," he expresses.

"*Do tell,*" I say in an exaggerated tone as I lean forward and place my elbows on the kitchen island.

He continues. "It's given me some time to think. I think... I need to work on my dancing, I should probably do some research on how to chase off a possum, and I definitely need to learn how to cook before humiliating myself anymore."

After Cole and I clean up the kitchen and have a few spare minutes, we decide to go hang out with the rest of the family. Aside from the kids building sandcastles, nearly everyone is scattered on the back patio of the Old Lavender House.

Dalton's parents are both stationed at the grill, and their food smells delicious. There's a crowd sitting around a small bonfire in Adirondack chairs, and everyone chuckles at a joke my dad made.

I find an open seat next to McCall and sit down. "What'd I miss?"

"For starters, there was an awful game of charades between Malik and the kids. Malik tried to replicate an erupting volcano, and it was *not* a pretty sight. Since then, your dad has been sharing volcano jokes and making everyone '*lava out loud*'."

"Oh gosh," I remark. "He's always trying to come up with puns."

"I can tell. Each one made Grandma Rose '*erupt*' with laughter."

"They sure did!" My grandmother calls out from a few seats over. By the tears that have formed in her eyes, it's clear that she's been laughing for quite some time.

I rest my head back on the chair and take it all in. Waves roll onto the shore, laughter echoes, Juniper is covered in sand, attempting to make 'snow angels', and I watch as Saylor's sand castle comes crumbling down. Cole is sitting across from me, engrossed in conversation with the guys.

Minutes pass in a peaceful blur until McCall nudges me. "I forgot to ask," she begins, "how's the chicken coming along?"

I sit up in my chair with a jolt. "*The chicken!*" I quietly mutter under my breath. "Oh my goodness, it's in the oven. I need to go check on it."

"*Still?*" Her attempt at whispering is louder than mine, and a few heads turn toward us. I smile politely at them, doing my best to hide the panic that's beginning to flash across my face. I'm unsure of how much time has passed.

I crouch down beside Cole's chair and explain, "I'm going to check on the chicken. I forgot it was in the oven."

His eyes go wide. "Shoot! That makes two of us." He turns to Malik and Dalton. "I'll be back in a few minutes."

"No worries," Dalton shrugs. "We'll be over there shortly. Malik's going to show me something on his dad's car."

Cole and I begin our walk back to the house, but I notice that McCall and the guys aren't far behind.

As I'm sliding open the back door, I hear the all-too-familiar screech of the smoke alarm. "Didn't they just get this stupid thing fixed?"

Cole squeezes past me and rushes into the kitchen. "They did!" he shouts over the ruckus as I scurry beside him.

If there's no more phantom beeping, then what does....

Cole swings open the oven door. Beneath the cloud of dark smoke, I watch as the bright, orange flames erupt.

Chapter 21

THE GRAND REVEAL

The heat immediately escapes, causing me to jump back into a state of panic.

Cole slams the oven door to contain the fire and quickly pushes a few buttons to shut it *off.* "This is not a false alarm!" he yells.

"Oh my gosh!" I exclaim as I hear McCall's loud shriek resonate behind me.

Cole rummages through the cabinets, frantically opening and closing each one. I rush to join him and find a fire extinguisher tucked away under the sink. With the uncertainty of how to use it, I quickly pass it over to him. He hesitates, reassessing the situation. With the oven door closed, the orange hues begin to fade, and the fire extinguisher may not be necessary after all. Even though the flames have dissipated, the smell of smoke and fire has leaked out into the air.

Malik, McCall, and Dalton are opening the downstairs windows. With Cole watching to make sure the fire is contained, I join the others, helping to let the fresh air in and the hazy air out. I slide open the double doors and use a spare flowerpot to keep them propped open.

The noise and commotion must have been loud enough next door for Aunt Sheryl to come strolling inside. "Why is this darn thing beeping again after I—" She stops, presumably smelling the hint of smoke in the air. Her tone of voice that follows is even more ear piercing than the smoke alarm. "What on Earth is going on in here?"

"Well…" I warily begin, "we had a slight mishap."

"This smells way worse than a *slight mishap*!"

Cole speaks up, "Don't worry; everything is under control now! There was a little fire but—"

"*Fire?*" Aunt Sheryl screams. With her high octaves, I'm expecting the rest of our crew to rush over in a state of urgency.

"Yes, *but*," I say, lifting a finger before she can scream about anything else, "the fire is out. We'll come up with another idea for dinner."

"And Finley and I will clean the oven!" Cole offers with a charming smile. "It'll look brand new by the time we're finished."

The smoke alarm finally stops the warning that, *for once,* was justifiable. Aunt Sheryl takes a deep breath in and exhales with her eyes fixated on the high ceiling.

Without making eye contact with any of us, she calmly expresses, "When I return, please let this house be in one piece." She spins on her heels and walks out the back door.

"Well," I sigh after her exit, "Cole and I are not to be trusted in the kitchen."

"Noted," McCall states with a bewildered expression.

Cole walks over and holds his phone out to me. The name of a restaurant is written across the top of his screen. "Plan B?"

I chuckle at his quick solution. "Sounds great to me."

Oohs and *ahhs* are expressed at the grand reveal of the Brays' grilled chicken. From the looks alone, their dinner is well-deserving of praise. It is cooked to golden perfection with a honey glaze and topped with a mix of rosemary and thyme. They're also serving grilled vegetables, whereas the thought of making a side dish didn't even cross our minds.

On the other hand, our chicken did not even make it to the table. It's inedible and has been tossed to the bottom of the trash can in a fiery, failed attempt.

Eddie shoots us a look as he reveals our dish. Nearly everyone has heard about our epic dinner fail, yet Cole and I do our best to not let our defeat show. We figured that if we look innocent and in love, my family would forgive us for nearly sending the beach manor up in flames. We hold hands, and I am uncomfortably resting my head on his shoulder in an attempt to enhance our facade.

"And from the bride's household is…" Eddie draws out his words and lifts the cover, revealing slices of pizza on a silver platter.

A low murmur of giggles follows our reveal. It's quite the opposite reaction from *oohs* and *ahhs*, yet I can't help but join the quiet fits of laughter. At the end of the day, Cole and I can at least say that we *tried* to make chicken. I'd like to think it would've turned out just like Margot's… but ours sadly didn't 'mar-*go*' as planned when we forgot about it in the oven.

Pizza is what Aunt Sheryl stated to Cole was '*absolutely not*' a meal on our first day here. The irony just makes me laugh a little harder.

Growing up, we typically sat in alphabetical order during school functions. While we were never directly side by side, with my last name being Brooks and Cole's being Baxter, we sat close enough. *Close enough to…* stick our tongues out at each other during our Kindergarten graduation and give proud thumbs-ups as we received our high school diplomas.

It appears nothing has changed. Cole sits across from me at the dinner table tonight, sticking his tongue out at me. His tussled brown hair looks the same as it did all those years ago.

Jokingly, I blow a kiss to him. My mom shoots me a confused half-smile as her eyes dart back and forth between the two of us.

Laughter and chatter flow around the table, just as harmonious as the breeze in my hair. With so many people sitting at the long table, it's hard to catch all the conversations. Uncle Malcolm is talking to my dad about his job. We have no plans of ever coming clean about his car—even McCall hasn't said a word. She turns to me, and we delve into a discussion about our future colleges. Malik says something a few seats down that makes Cole burst into laughter. As per usual, Sierra and Dalton look head over heels for one another as they're chatting.

I bite into a slice of pizza, secretly glad that I get to eat this instead. I had a few bites of their delicious grilled chicken, but pizza will always remind me of my childhood.

It feels very fitting to eat it now as I'm spending time with my cousins whom I grew up with and the boy next door... who's sticking his tongue out at me. *Again.*

Chapter 22

CLOSE

Cole and I have always been close by association. We celebrated every birthday together, even once the party games and piñatas turned into bonfires at the lake. We had weekly family dinners and game nights. The two of us being *close* has always been easy.

We were only separated by twenty-seven steps from my front door to his—twenty if we ran. At times, thirty feet of string attached to cups on both ends linked our second-story bedroom windows. We crammed beside one another, playing in our five-by-five treehouse.

Even though we have always been close by association, *we're now close by choice.* In some ways, it's not the same as it was back then.

As everyone begins to head inside after dinner, we sneak the final slices of pizza from the box and dart to the gazebo. I think we are faster in this moment than during any race that was held earlier today.

Cole's hand hits one of the posts on the gazebo with a *smack*. "I win."

"We definitely were *not* racing," I say with pointed eyes. "If that were the case, *I* would've won."

"Do you want a rematch?"

"Not now, but one day," I exclaim with a wink.

In the opening of the gazebo, both of us plop down onto the top of the steps. We sit with our backs pressed against the posts. A pepperoni falls onto my lap, and I silently hope that no others fell along the way. One possum encounter was more than enough for me.

Interrupting the silence, Cole begins to chuckle. "I can't believe we caught the food on fire."

"I can!" I proclaim. "They should have never put us in charge. The two of us cooking dinner without any adult supervision was practically a recipe for disaster."

"Agreed," he notes. "I thought I was going to singe my eyebrows off when I opened the oven door."

I snicker midway through another bite. "I'm so glad you didn't. Our time here has been quite entertaining, but that would have been the real icing on the cake. I can't believe how fast this week is going."

"I know," he agrees. "We only have what... five days left until we go home?"

I pause, counting through the days on my fingers. "Sadly," I confirm.

We hold eye contact, and neither of us says anything for a moment. The moonlight reflects from the water, illuminating Cole. It shows his hair's hidden curls that get more prominent with the summertime humidity.

There's a gleam in his eyes from the light, and although I can't see the exact shade now, I know his eyes are chocolate brown. I think I see a shooting star zip by in the sky, but I convince myself it's only an airplane in the distance. I've never experienced a meteor shower with impeccable timing—timing that perfectly lines up with my thoughts fixated on the boy in front of me. Some would say it's a good sign, but I only take it to mean that my imagination is way too overactive. One too many romance novels could do that to you.

"In five days, things will go back to normal." His words almost sound uncertain. "We'll go back to living under two roofs, I won't get to hold your hand," he chuckles slowly, "and we'll be the same old Finley and Cole we've always been."

The version of Finley and Cole who were close by association… not necessarily by choice.

"I kind of like the new Finley and Cole," I point out with a bittersweet tone coating my words. "It's been fun—even when you forced me into the ocean or when we got close to sending the venue up in smoke."

He chuckles. "We need to stay away from anything that could result in flames, but it has been fun. I'm genuinely enjoying myself."

"Even though you're staying in a room with my ex's name on the door and in a house filled with my slightly insane family?"

"Oh, especially that! They've been a highlight for sure," he notes. "With your family, you never know what crazy thing will happen next. I think that's what makes it so fun. Four days ago my mom was planning a week of shopping for dorm essentials against my will and now you've roped me into a week-long vacation an hour and a half away from home. If it means avoiding shopping for bedsheets, pillow shams, and shower shoes, I'll play my part as your Lover Boy any day of the week."

"My *Lover Boy?*" I laugh and playfully push him away. "You may need to step up your act a notch or two before you consider yourself my Lover Boy."

"Ugh!" Cole scoffs sarcastically. "Is holding your hand not enough?" He says as he scoots closer to me. Cautiously, he outstretches his hand. I jokingly push it away.

He rests his hand on the top of my knee and this time... I don't object.

I shrug with a smile still peeking through. "I'm just saying...." *In reality, I have no clue what I'm saying.* I can hardly gather my thoughts over the flirtatious turn of this conversation.

At the gazebo, it is only us and the stars. Everyone else has gone in for the night. We don't have to fake anything for anyone, and yet here we are... *close.* As we're sitting snug between the opening of the steps, it reminds me of a more grownup version of our treehouse. After all, we are just a *slightly* more grown-up version of those kids.

I watch as the rare glimmer of a comet zips through the indigo sky yet again, but it's surely just another figment of my imagination... *right?*

Unless perfect timing truly does exist.

WEDNESDAY

3 Days Until the Wedding

WEDNESDAY *playlist*

- traitor ——————————— Olivia Rodrigo
- Happily ———————————— One Direction
- Looking At Me Like That ————— Vance Joy
- Looking at Me ——————— Sabrina Carpenter
- She Will Be Loved ———————— Maroon 5
- WHERE WE ARE ————————— The Lumineers
- You Belong With Me (*Taylor's Version*) —————
  —————————————— Taylor Swift
- Feels Like ————————— Gracie Abrams
- Nonsense ——————— Sabrina Carpenter
- That Feeling ———————— HARBOUR
- Flowers in Your Hair —————— The Lumineers
- Love Like That ————————— Phillip Phillips
- Anyone Else ————————— Joshua Bassett
- Sweet Nothing ———————— Taylor Swift
- Boardwalk ———————————— Vance Joy
- All Of The Girls You Loved Before — Taylor Swift
- Young Lovers Do ————————— Tilly W
- If I Fall ——————————— Nick Jonas

Chapter 23

REFLECT & FIND

Since my breakup with Jesse, I feel as though I've had a lot of time to reflect. Not only have I had a lot of time to replay *that* moment of Jesse kissing another girl on Valentine's Day in my head, but I've also had a lot of time to ponder it all.

When you're in a relationship with someone, it almost feels like you become *one*. If someone were to think about me, they'd probably think of him as well. I was tied to him in every possible way, and by the end of our relationship, I nearly felt like I lost my light while living in the shadow of his.

When his friends invited him to a party, I was there and trailing behind him as a default invite. He sat next to me at all of Wren's plays. Even the simple things like running errands or getting lunch, we did together. We'd text one another each night before we fell asleep and messaged 'good morning' as soon as our eyes were open. We shared our schedules with one another and knew every little detail such as upcoming doctors' appointments. While in a relationship with Jesse, I began to feel like I was losing my privacy.

I felt like I was losing myself too.

Everything I was perfectly capable of doing alone always resulted in an extra person accompanying me. Even so, it wasn't always a bad thing. Our relationship wasn't always rocky. There were plenty of times that trips together to Mountain Mart became the highlight of my day, times when a joke he said made me laugh hysterically, and times I was truly and irrevocably... *happy*.

Then I felt like I lost that too.

After *that* moment in the school hallway, I did my best to pull myself together over the next few days. I told myself that I was over *him*. However, there were some things that I couldn't get over—the memories we shared and the feeling that I had lost myself along with my personality. I almost wasn't sure how to be happy without my second half being there to complete me. And I *hated* that.

Trips to Mountain Mart felt lonely, drives to pick up lunch were silent, and I showed up to parties alone— or more often than not, I avoided them altogether.

After a while of secretly moping, I was sick of relying on him for my own happiness. Instead of waiting around for the void to fill, I began to shift things in my life. I found things that made me happy, and I did them at every opportunity.

Instead of letting myself sit alone in my bedroom, I would drive to the lake and enjoy one of my favorite pastimes. I watched the sunset as the colors bloomed in the sky, reminding me that not all endings are bad.

My trips to Wonderland Books became more frequent than ever, and I flew through books, devouring every plot twist and cheesy romance line. I got lost in the pages of worlds other than mine and was reminded that plot twists sometimes need to happen for a happily ever after.

I filled my silent rides to Mountain Mart with my favorite music. I blasted songs through the speakers that Jesse would've *never* allowed to be played while riding with him. I sang my heart out to *traitor* by Olivia Rodrigo and shed a few tears. Before long, I danced my way through One Direction and didn't think twice about Jesse.

I frequently went out for ice cream, called my girlfriends more, and tried to learn how to knit—yet I failed miserably at my attempt at a new hobby. I laced up my tennis shoes for more family hikes, went out to lunch with friends I had abandoned before, and most importantly, found my happiness. As cheesy as it sounds, *I found myself again.* After the journey, I decided that those things weren't going to change. Sure, I'd eventually have another boyfriend one day, but I wasn't going to change for him—or anyone else.

By finding myself, I realized that I never wanted to lose myself ever again.

Chapter 24

SIXTH SENSE

This morning has been slow in the Hollow Oak house, so I toss on a bathing suit, finally putting one to good use. I tie my hair up into a messy bun and grab my current read from the bedside table.

With the ocean now in my line of view and the manor behind me, I throw my bag onto one of the available Adirondack chairs and spread out my beach towel on the sand. Lying down, I open my book and let myself get lost in the pages.

The setting around me is superb, blue skies with the sun hidden behind a cloud and the relaxing hum of waves as they roll onto the shore.

I'm seven chapters in when Cole appears beside me in the sand. "Want to go on a walk?"

I finish the sentence I'm currently reading, then I glance up at him.

Before I can respond he crouches down and says, "I'll let you finish your chapter first, if that's what you were about to say."

I smile as I respond, "Sure, I'll walk. I only have a few pages left of this chapter."

"No rush." He plops down, sitting fully on the sand.

"Here, I can scoot over," I offer as I inch to the edge of the towel and attempt to make enough room for him. A lock of my blonde hair falls down in front of my face.

"Thanks." Cole lays on his stomach beside me. His elbow rests against mine, and neither of us makes an effort to move.

I read the words on the page, scanning the black ink that contrasts with the white. Then I read the paragraph for a second time, and once more. It's not a scene that is leaving me speechless—in my book, anyway. I'm having to reread it because I can't focus on the story in front of me. With every word I read, I see Cole in my peripheral. His eyes are studying my face, and it takes a lot to keep my eyes from lifting off the page and meeting his.

Cole reaches over and tucks the loose strand of hair behind my ear. Despite the hot sun that beats down, his touch sends a nervous chill all the way down to my toes.

I turn to face him, finally making eye contact. He clears his throat and is looking just as flustered as I feel.

"Don't look now, but your Grandma Rose is watching," he whispers.

"Ah," I manage to say. "Good call with the hair then. For a second, I thought you were just being sweet."

"We have to keep up the act, right?" His smiling eyes don't falter their gaze with mine.

Just barely smiling, I nod. I do my best to go back to reading.

I've always been comfortable around Cole. I don't have to put up any sort of front. My hair could be flying in a million different directions, and I wouldn't bother to smooth down a single strand. I don't think about what I'm saying beforehand; I just let the words roll off my tongue.

Yet, as this week continues, it feels as though new layers are being unwrapped. Yes, I'm still comfortable, but I'm also hyperaware. I'm hyperaware when his eyes are on mine or on me, as they are now. I'm hyperaware of the words that come tumbling from my mouth and my body language. The locks of hair that have recently been tucked behind my ear feel as though they weigh a ton, and this only further proves this new sixth sense of mine.

I tell myself it's because it's all pretend. Maybe I'm not hyper-focused on Cole but rather on the people around us. Perhaps I'm focusing on how they're perceiving our quote-unquote relationship and whether or not they're believing it.

That has to be it, right? I ponder. Cole and I have been around one another our whole lives, and this newfound arrangement is the only thing that's changed between us. Yet even as I say these words in my head, I'm not one hundred percent sure I perceive them as the truth. I'm not believing that's *all* that has changed.

With a quick inhale, I grab my bookmark, place it between the pages, and shut the cover of my paperback.

"Done already?" he asks.

"I was at a good stopping point."

Truthfully, I have no recollection of anything I just read. The past five minutes of scanning the page have felt like an eternity. I can only remember the reality of being on high alert, fighting a flushed smile, and feeling his presence once again... very close to mine.

"So," he begins after a moment, "What's your book about?"

As I gather my things and give him a quick summary, I notice that my Grandma Rose isn't anywhere in sight. It's just the two of us in our own little world.

"Do you have any plans for today?" he asks a few minutes later as we walk barefoot along the cool water's edge.

"Umm," I pause to think. "No, not that I know of. Why? What's up?"

He grins mischievously. "Nothing really. I'm just thinking about doing... *something*. No need to be concerned."

I glare at him, narrowing my eyes. "That sentence alone concerns me."

Chapter 25

FAMILY ANTICS

After returning to the house, Cole ran into town to grab a few things. I opted to stay behind, spend more time with my family, and dive headfirst into the Hollow Oak antics.

Sierra and Dalton are curled up on the couch, taking selfies and giggling at the ridiculous filters that cover their faces. Blaire is baking yet again—this time a lemon pound cake. Cole and I scrubbed the oven last night until it looked normal and unscathed... although I can still smell a hint of burnt chicken in the air. Hopefully, it's just a figment of my imagination since no one else has mentioned the scent.

McCall and I sit cross-legged on the living room rug as we play with Juniper. She waddles between the two of us, giggling as we play peek-a-boo. Even after the tenth *"Peek-a-boo!"*, it's just as hilarious to her as it was the first time, only now she's figured out the pattern of our game.

Ryder comes rushing down the stairs with his hand securing the top hat on his head. A long, black cape is draped over his shoulders. "Ladies and gentlemen!" he calls, entering the room with style.

"Oh, here we go," I chuckle. I bought him a magic kit for his birthday last month, and he has since become an aspiring magician. He's practiced consistently back home and sadly, even after a month, he still isn't great. Despite that, he is still determined to put on the best show for everyone in Sunrise Beach.

"Ooh!" Aunt Kira cheers from the couch.

Ryder throws his arm up in the air and pauses for dramatic effect. The other hand doesn't loosen its grip on his hat. "It is I, *The Ravishing Ryder*! Please take your seats and be prepared to witness the *best* magic show of your life!" He walks over to Caroline who's sitting at the kitchen island. "Would you like to be my volunteer?"

Caroline chuckles. "Sure thing, little dude!" She stands and follows him back to the center of the room. At this point, Ryder has gathered the attention of everyone downstairs and has a full audience.

"Assistant!" he yells and loudly claps his hands twice.

Saylor, my five-year-old sister, walks into the room, dragging a large black bag that's nearly her size.

Ryder turns to her. "Can I have my cards, please?"

Wordlessly, she reaches into the bag and pulls out a few items—none of them being a deck of cards. She continues to shuffle around in the bag with no luck. Caroline reaches down and grabs them almost immediately. "Here you go," she whispers with a gentle smile as she holds them out to Ryder.

He takes them and smiles so big that you would think he was just kissed by a princess. Awkwardly, he fans out the cards in his small hands. "Pick a card, ma'am. Any card!"

Caroline happily grabs one from the center of the deck.

"Now, show the audience!"

She holds out the King of Hearts.

Ryder readjusts his top hat. He grabs a random card from the stack. "Is this your card?" He speaks in the tone of a true magician, loud and enticing. The card he is holding is a five of diamonds.

"No… not quite," Caroline says.

"How about this?" He holds up an eight of clubs.

She grimaces, shaking her head.

Everyone is holding in a quiet chuckle but encouraging him each time he gets closer. This is not your typical deck of cards, as it's missing the majority of options. Before long, he has repeated most of the cards since they are duplicated throughout the deck.

He flips another card over. "Is *this* it?"

Caroline cheers. "Yes! That's the one!"

A round of applause echoes around the large room. After a few more tricks that don't take nearly as long, Ryder goes on to show everyone his grand finale. Saylor hands him his black and white wand, and he ever so carefully takes his hat off. With his poorly pronounced attempt at the magic words, he yells out, "*Abba-abba-kadavabra!*"

He reaches into his hat and pulls out a fluffy, stuffed rabbit. The cheer for this trick is louder than the others, possibly because he did a great job of *not* letting his hat fall off... and he succeeded on his first attempt.

"Wooo!" I call, joining the others.

Ryder gives his final bow before heading back upstairs. Saylor bows and begins to make her way up the stairs as well. As she carries the large bag with her, it hits every step with a *thud.*

I'm holding Juniper in my arms, so McCall rushes over to help Saylor with the bag—just as she did a few days ago when helping me with my suitcase.

The timer in the kitchen sounds, and Blaire excitedly scurries to the oven. As she opens the door, the aroma of lemons fills the air. This scent is *much* more welcome than that of charred chicken.

Grandma Rose rises from her spot on the couch and walks toward the kitchen. Just then, the front door creaks open. I can't see the door or the mystery guest from where I'm sitting, but I hear my grandmother's voice echo as she exclaims, "Aww! Now, aren't you just the sweetest thing? Finley!" I stand at the mention of my name. Heading into the kitchen, she winks at me. "I guess romance isn't dead after all."

"Hey now!" My Grandpa Joe shouts, obviously offended.

"Just saying." She shrugs innocently.

With just a few steps, I see who's standing inside the doorway. To my surprise, Cole is holding a large bouquet of flowers in his hand.

"Hi." He smiles and outstretches the bouquet to me.

"Hi...?" I question as I take them. "Why the *flowers*?" I try to give him a sly look without the others noticing.

"I have something planned for us today. Would you join me?"

Chapter 26

THE BROKEN RULE or THE FOLLOWED RULE

I rush upstairs, set the flowers on the dresser, and make a mental note to place them in a vase once we return from… wherever we're going. I'm headed out the bedroom door when I notice my reflection in the mirror.

Even though our date is strictly for show—I shouldn't go out looking like this. I pause and quickly run my fingers through the tangled strands of my hair, watching as they transform into calm, blonde waves. I dig through my suitcase until I find my makeup bag. With fears of the pesky pimple returning, I had zero plans of wearing makeup before the wedding. However, this calls for an exception. I grab a makeup brush, dust the lightest amount of bronzer onto my cheekbones, and stroke dark mascara through my lashes, making my green eyes pop. I settle with a simplistic look and finally leave the room.

"Finley!" McCall stops me as I'm on my way out. Saylor and Ryder must have kept her occupied since she offered to help them. "Where are you rushing off to?" She leans in closer, inspecting my face. "Do you have fake eyelashes on?"

I inch backward. "No, just mascara." I pause, feeling a brighter blush on my cheeks now than I did in front of everyone downstairs. "I'm going with Cole *onadate.*" I rush the last half of my sentence and all the words blend into one.

"Huh?" she questions. "You're going on a *lake*? Where is there a lake nearby?"

I chuckle. "No, not a lake—I'm going on a *date*, but I'm not sure where."

"Aww, how sweet!" She gives me a quick hug and sends me on my way. "Enjoy!"

Cole waits for me at the bottom of the stairs with a smile. "You ready?" he asks as I reach him.

"Yep," I nod quickly.

We're almost out the front door when my mom chimes in, "You two have fun!"

My dad interjects, "Not too much fun. I know where you live, Cole!"

Cole and I both chuckle as we reach the front porch.

"So," I start, "Where are we headed on this grand date of ours?"

"You'll see," he says with a smirk as he opens the passenger door for me to climb in.

After driving for about five minutes, we stop in a secluded area of the beach. The warm and inviting summer breeze helps to calm my nerves—although I truly have no *real* reason to be nervous at all.

In front of us is a long boardwalk that stretches over the sun-kissed water. The waves crash against the large rocks, occasionally splashing water onto the wooden planks. I keep an eye on the cracks as I follow Cole's lead down the boardwalk.

"As much as I appreciate this," I begin, "You know we don't have to keep up the dramatics right now."

Cole waves his hand in the air. "No, no, no. I believe my exact words were '*I'm going to sell the crap out of this fake relationship*'. That's exactly what I'm doing."

I roll my eyes, yet I can't help but smile. "You're ridiculous. Who exactly are you trying to sell it to? There's no one else around."

"I mean, well… I plan to make the most of it."

"Oh, do you?" I question further.

"Yep." He nods proudly. "I also plan to make this your most memorable relationship yet."

I chuckle. "Overachiever much?"

"Eh, Jesse set the bar pretty low."

My initial gasp turns into a quiet laugh. "Thanks for bringing him up—and on my first date since, nonetheless. You're already making this pretty memorable, aren't you?"

"I'm sorry, but he was just..." he pauses, trying to find the right words. "He was a jerk, Fin. Maybe you don't have the best taste in guys."

"I chose you," I say matter-of-factly.

He's quick to shoot back a joke of his own. "In your lottery of choices for a fake boyfriend over Otto Jones? I'm truly flattered."

"Oh, you've had some real winners too," I reply sarcastically. "It's hard to forget about the time when Amy ghosted you because—"

"Okay, okay!" Cole swiftly turns and grabs my hand in an attempt to make me stop talking about *his* failed relationships. "I get your point, but I think that's enough chitchat about our exes. This is *our* date, after all."

"Sure thing, *Babe,* although you started it."

We continue to walk down the boardwalk and even though Cole grabbed my hand so I'd stop talking, neither of us is letting go.

"Oh!" I practically yell. I turn to him with a pointed finger. "I have a bone to pick with you, Mr."

"*Really?* What's that?"

"You broke a rule today. You brought me flowers after I explicitly told you not to!"

"But!" He lifts a finger back at me. "I also took you on a date, which *was* a rule... so I think that makes it even."

"You think that one broken rule and one followed rule cancel each other out?"

"That's exactly how it works."

"Yeah, okay," I tease.

"I'm just joking," he says with a smile. "But in other news... did it work?"

I furrow my brows. "Hmm?"

"Did you fall in love with me? After all... I *did* bring you flowers."

I laugh, feeling the rise and fall in my chest. "Oh, Cole Baxter...." *Clearly* joking, I admit, "Thanks to those tulips, I think I'm falling head over heels in love with you."

Sarcastically, he pumps his fist in the air. His other hand stays laced through mine.

As we're nearing the end of the boardwalk, I say in a more sincere tone, "I know I told you not to, but thank you for the flowers. It really means a lot to me... and they're pretty." I glance down, watching the wooden slats pass as I try to hide the blush rising in my cheeks.

With a nonchalant shrug, he says, "You're welcome. I'm glad you liked the flowers, because..."

I look up in front of me as we round the corner, and I immediately notice the cream-colored blanket that's laid out at the end of the boardwalk. A picnic basket is set in the center and each corner of the blanket is adorned with small bouquets of *flowers*. There's a beautiful variety in small, glass vases. Each vase holds a different kind—white daisies, red roses, pink peonies, and lastly yellow tulips that match the ones I have sitting on my dresser.

"*Cole*...." I breathe out, my eyes beginning to water. I could blame it on the wind, but I know that's not the case. It's the thought that no one has ever done anything like this for me.

"As I said, I have to make the most of this week. Fake relationships only happen once—it's best to make it memorable."

"I'll never forget this." I smile before wrapping my arms around him in a tight hug.

Chapter 27

A MYTH

I don't recall ever feeling this type of nervous energy—the kind that makes you pinch yourself to ensure this moment is real. This exciting glimmer of nerves stems from sharing a special moment with that special someone.

Without a doubt, there was *something* between Jesse and me. There was *something* that made me want to spend time with him each day… although I don't think I ever felt that true *spark*. Looking back, it was more of an ember that we clung to.

I liked to believe that the electrifying nerves caused by love were strictly myths to sell romance novels. Perhaps someone wrote the story of the protagonist with a stomach full of flittering butterflies. It stuck with the rest of the world and made them desire that same feeling—*myself included*. While dating Jesse, I never had the butterfly feeling, therefore I had to come up with *something* to suffice. I needed something to make myself believe that I was actually *in* love and not just saying '*I love you*'.

Yet now, I'm on a quote-unquote date with someone I never imagined. We're sitting on a blanket that overlooks the ocean and... I feel a flutter in my stomach. Maybe it's the sparkling water that Cole packed for the picnic, or maybe it's just my anxiety... but maybe it *is* the butterflies.

Perhaps they're not a myth after all.

Chapter 28

JUST POSSIBLY...

When it comes to Cole Baxter, I thought I knew everything.

I know that he likes his coffee loaded with creamer. When we had to leave for school before the break of dawn, Cole always drove, so I volunteered to supply the coffee and breakfast. Granted, it was usually just a pack of doughnuts or toaster waffles.

He always double-knots his shoelaces. One untied lace caused his football team to lose a game when he tripped and fell before making it into the end zone. That was eleven years ago, and I have only seen double knots since.

The list could go on. The blue bag of *Doritos* has always been his favorite. Even though he won't admit it, I think he secretly loves *The Vampire Diaries*. In middle school, he played basketball just to make his dad happy by 'following in his footsteps'. The only song he has downloaded on his phone is *Everybody Wants to Rule the World*, and it blasts out by default nearly every time he starts his car.

Yet being here with him now, it feels as though we're meeting for the first time.

Perhaps there's always been this side of Cole that I've yet to see all these years. Maybe our arrangement just brought out the version of him that unapologetically sweeps you off your feet and into the ocean, opens car doors, sets up a surprise picnic, takes full blame for sending the food up in flames, and brings you flowers in front of your family.

A part of me understands that our arrangement is fake. It's completely for show. Realistically, he only swept me off my feet to play his role as my boyfriend, opened doors to seem romantic in front of others, and took me on a date to follow through with our rule.

But then there's the part of me that is privately hoping that it's *not* fake. The entire notion is complete nonsense, but I can't seem to keep my thoughts at bay. What if in some reality... it could become true? What if it already is?

I haven't fallen for Cole Baxter.... I won't fall for Cole Baxter.

Although... I will forever remember this week when I may have just possibly... begun to *trip*.

THURSDAY
2 Days Until the Wedding

THURSDAY *playlist*

- Heaven Falls/Fall On Me —————— Surfaces
- My Type ————————————— Saint Motel
- I'm Good ————————— The Mowgli's
- Love Song ———————————— Sara Bareilles
- Sweet Talk ————————————— Saint Motel
- Everything Has Changed (*Taylor's Version*) ———— ————————————— Taylor Swift, Ed Sheeran
- Sweetheart (*Unreleased*) ————— Joshua Bassett
- Satellite —————————————— Harry Styles
- this is what falling in love feels like ———— JVKE
- gold rush ———————————— Taylor Swift
- I Want You to Want Me ————— Cheap Trick
- Like Gold ————————————— Vance Joy
- Just for a Moment ———————————————— ————————— Olivia Rodrigo, Joshua Bassett
- We Made It ——————————— Louis Tomlinson
- Glitch ————————————— Taylor Swift
- Different ——————————— Joshua Bassett
- Kiss Me While You Can (Unreleased) ———— ————————————————— Joshua Bassett
- I Think He Knows ——————— Taylor Swift

Chapter 29

PICTURESQUE PICNIC

McCall and I stayed up a little later last night, scrolling through Pinterest. Crammed together in my bed, we searched for a special dessert that we could surprise Sierra with for her bridesmaid picnic later this afternoon.

After half an hour of being indecisive, we finally chose a design—a round cake with white frosting and sliced strawberries on top.

Now, picking a design and actually making it look similar are *vastly* different. With the house low on supplies, we borrow my mom's car to pick up the ingredients and return quickly so we have time to bake and let it cool.

This endeavor is smooth sailing compared to our previous time spent in this kitchen. Today, we're actually able to fill the comfortable silence with music.

Most of the guests are outside enjoying the beautiful weather and getting to know Dalton's family and friends. Aunt Sheryl, Sierra, Blaire, and Aunt Kira have gone a few towns over to look for last-minute wedding supplies.

Late last night while Aunt Kira was helping to organize the decorations, she realized that three centerpieces are missing. First thing this morning, they set off to search the nearby stores. They quickly returned and Aunt Sheryl was frantic. She made another pot of coffee for the road while explaining that they had no luck finding candlesticks or tall glass vases that matched the rest of the decor. This urged them to continue their search four towns over.

I pour the cake batter from the mixing bowl into the round cake pans. Just seconds later, the oven reaches three hundred and fifty degrees and beeps.

I turn to McCall, who's slicing strawberries. "I'll let *you* handle the oven this time."

"Good idea," she chuckles.

In order to keep a watchful eye on the timer and cake, we stick around in the kitchen, chatting. After it bakes to perfection and cools off, it's time for the fun part. With supplies laid out in front of us, we begin decorating. Wren joins us, places a big glob of icing on the center of the cake, and smoothes it with a small spatula. As the cake is nearly finished, Sierra and her *Centerpiece Search Party* walk through the front door.

I can hear glass clanking together as Sierra happily lifts the bags into the air. "We found some!"

Aunt Sheryl plops onto the couch with a sigh of relief. "We did! They aren't an exact match, but they're pretty close. I think they'll be fine."

Aunt Kira leans in between McCall and me. "It took some *major* convincing for Sheryl to believe that," she whispers.

The three of us giggle lightly so no one hears—pointedly, Aunt Sheryl.

Blaire strolls into the kitchen, taking a peek at our cake. "Ooh, this looks good!"

Wren smiles proudly. She's become close to Blaire this week—especially in the kitchen as she bakes. "Thanks! Finley and McCall made the cake for the bridal picnic. I'm just helping to decorate it."

Sierra takes a seat at the island. "Aww! You guys didn't have to do that, although it *does* look delicious. I can't wait to dig in!" Caroline and Peyton join us as we snack on the leftover strawberries and icing until both containers are empty and it's nearly time to head to the nail salon.

After hours of spa treatment and mani-pedis, we are finally free of the salon smell. The bridesmaids all decided to get a shade of light lavender ahead of time. Sierra's nails are perfectly fit for a bride—a classy, light beige with white French tips. I shoot my mom a quick text, letting her know that we're on our way. This serves as their heads-up so they can finish the picnic display before we get back. Sierra is aware that the picnic is happening, but Aunt Sheryl wants the setup to be a surprise.

As we walk through the doors of Hollow Oak, my mom and Aunt Sheryl rush toward us. "Hey, girls! Don't look out back just yet."

"Uhh, why not?" Sierra questions as she slides off her foam pedicure sandals.

"The picnic is set up, and I want us to all walk out together."

"Ooh, I can't wait!" Sierra beams.

My mom pulls me aside. "I thought you were going to message me with a heads-up when you left. We heard the car pull up the driveway, so Sheryl and I had to rush inside."

"I did!" I exclaim as I pull out my phone. **YOUR MESSAGE TO 'MOM' FAILED TO SEND,** is written across my screen. I lift it to show her. "Ugh, that's why you didn't see it. Sorry."

My mom sighs. "Ah, I think everyone has had bad luck with signal here all week."

I nod in agreement, thinking about our failed phone calls with no reception after the car broke down.

Now that everyone is ready, I grab the cake we made and head out the back door.

On the sand and near the brink of the shore, a picnic that is fit for a movie scene is set up. The table is low to the ground on a massive throw blanket. Plates and silverware line the table's edge, each accompanied by an empty etched glass. Pitchers sit in the center of the table, filled with ice water, lemonade, and champagne. Large trays are scattered on the table and overflowing with food. We have a large variety to choose from—a mix of fruits and vegetables, crackers, cheeses, meats, finger sandwiches, sugar cookies, and now our strawberry cake. Light greenery and pale lavender flowers fill the space between the trays. Solar-powered fairy lights are draped around us. Rows of throw pillows are arranged on the blanket and match everything perfectly.

I hear the camera shutter clicking as I notice Aunt Kira capturing everyone's reactions.

"This is beautiful!" Sierra exclaims as she runs to Aunt Sheryl, giving her a grateful hug. "Thank you, Mom!"

"Of course, Baby Girl." Aunt Sheryl beams proudly. While she can sometimes be dramatic or a little bit harsh, Aunt Sheryl's soft spot has always been Sierra —her *Baby Girl* whom she would put the world on pause for.

I take a seat on a purple, velvet pillow. McCall sits to my left, and Wren plops down to my right.

"Oh, geez," Peyton says, slowly crouching down on the other side of the table. She has one hand on her pregnant belly and the other bracing against the table to slowly get down. Through a deep breath, she says, "I may need help getting this big belly up later."

"You okay?" Caroline asks, helping her to ease onto the pillow.

Peyton's breathing turns steady. "Yeah, I'm good. Being pregnant has its moments for sure, but it's definitely worth it in the end."

I grab the knife from beside my plate and reach forward, making the first cut into our cake as I listen to their conversation.

Blaire eyes Sierra with a little smirk. "Have you and Dalton talked any more about kids?"

Sierra smiles softly. "Yeah, we've talked about it. One day, for sure."

Wren gasps. "I'm going to be an *aunt*?" She loudly squeals.

Chuckling, Sierra swats at her. "Shh! No time soon. I'm not pregnant right *now*, Wren. Don't get my mom's hopes up by screaming it across the whole town."

"But one day?" she pleads with big eyes.

"Hopefully one day," Sierra agrees. "And you'd be a cousin, silly—not an aunt."

"Eh, they can still call me Aunt Wren. Maybe Auntie Re-Re?"

"Sure thing."

I grin. "When the day comes, I can picture you with a lot of kids." Growing up, Sierra was always in charge when the adults did their grown-up things. She's the oldest of all the cousins, but she's also had a way with kids even when she was one herself.

"A *lot*?" She lifts her brows.

"I can see you with at least five," McCall chimes.

Sierra shakes her head. "Oh, there is *no* way! The thought of five little humans running around under my feet sounds way too overwhelming."

Caroline shoots her a look. "Whatever! You're the most laid-back person I know. I've been a bridesmaid six times and have never seen a bride so *chill*. Kids would be a breeze for you."

"I agree, Sierra. I almost picture you going full *Cheaper by the Dozen*." Blaire chuckles.

Sierra's eyes go wide. "Five is sounding like a piece of cake now."

I lift my glass into the air. "To whatever the future holds."

We all clink glasses as Sierra chuckles, shaking her head. "Let's get through my wedding first," she exclaims. "Then we can talk more about the possibility of my family growing."

Blaire lifts her hand, placing it beside her mouth. "*Twelve kids*," she whispers to no one in particular.

With the ocean as a backdrop to our picturesque picnic, we all laugh. I hear the click of the camera once again. Completely in the moment, we've all simultaneously forgotten that Aunt Kira has been perched off to the side all along.

Two magical picnics in two days.

Both were perfect—the food, the conversations, the memories, the smiles... *and the people.*

I only wish to have had a secret photographer last night—someone to capture the moments where I laughed at Cole's corny jokes and felt myself leaning into him. A photo to forever remember the time that I had the best (*fake*) date of my life.

Chapter 30

WHAT IF I DO?

I'm rounding the corner at the top of the stairs when all of a sudden—"*Boo!*" A voice jumps out at me.

I let out a shriek and instinctively lift my hands in front of me.

A bellowing laugh rings out, one that I recognize as Cole's. Playfully, I push him against the wall. "Rude," I chuckle.

"Like you have any room to talk. You practically knocked a picture frame off the wall when you shoved me," he jokes.

"You totally deserved that."

He nods in agreement. "True. How was your day with the girls? Did y'all gossip about me?"

"Hate to disappoint you, but we didn't. We had a relaxing time getting our nails done, and we came home to a beautiful brunch picnic," I explain. "Oh, get this—

McCall and I baked a cake *without* needing a fire extinguisher, and it actually turned out really good! I saved you a slice."

"Nice!" He gives me a high five. "I can't wait to try it."

"How was your day with the guys? Are you like, totally '*one of the bros*' now?" Even though Cole isn't a part of the official wedding party, Dalton invited him to go hang out.

"It was fun! We went axe throwing and then stopped for lunch at a barbecue place. The food was great, but my axe-throwing skills were *axe-cellent*."

I giggle. "You're such an idiot. I think you've spent too much time with my grandma this week."

"You know I like to make you laugh—even if I make a fool of myself in the process."

"You've always been good at that. Do you want to do something?"

"Like what?"

"I'm not sure yet. Just something." I shrug. "We've hardly seen each other all day."

"Uh oh," he warns with widening eyes. "We've spent a few days together, and after one morning apart, it sounds like you're getting attached to me."

"I am *not* getting attached—I'm just trying to make the most of our week."

"Sure thing, Sweetheart."

"Still not a fan of the nicknames," I note.

Mischievously, he grins. "Believe me, I know. They make your cheeks go red, and you start to become flustered."

I shake my head while clicking my tongue. "What a shame," I tease. "Yesterday, you brought me on such a grand date, and now you're doing things just to irritate me. Unbelievable." Even with my best efforts, a smile is beginning to form on my lips.

"I can't have you getting *too* attached," he jokes, or at least I *think* he's joking. Maybe all of this is still just as make-believe for him now as it was from the start.

"Don't worry, I won't forget about our expiration date." The joking tone in my voice matches his.

"So, what shall we do?"

I smirk, playfully responding. "I thought I was the one getting too attached."

He drops his head, almost hiding his smile from me. "I mean... I *did* come upstairs to see what *you* were doing."

I lift a finger. "Same rules apply to you too, Baxter. Don't go falling in love with me."

He leans against my doorframe, serious as can be as he asks, "And what if I do?"

I roll my eyes in an attempt to fight that familiar bubbling feeling. The butterfly myth is once again proving to be factual. As I walk past him and into my room, I mutter, "Um, I'll be out in a second; I need to change real quick." Without another word, I shut the door. Not only do I need to change into something more comfortable, but I also need to change this conversation before I say something I'm sure to regret—something that's bound to embarrass me.

No matter my current feelings, the ending for Cole and I will remain the same. We don't have rules to break, we have rules to follow—*and our inevitable breakup is Rule #1*.

As I dig through my suitcase that I've been too stubborn to unpack, I search for a more casual outfit. I certainly couldn't bear to stand in the hallway any longer as I practically flirted with Cole—as he flirted with me. *Right? Isn't that what just happened?* The last time I was in the 'flirting' world, I was barely fifteen, and I *clearly* haven't been in a fake relationship before now. I feel slightly clueless. It's like we're actors who are terrible at their job—or possibly wonderful at it? It's blurred lines of what's real and what's for show… even when we're the only two people around.

I sigh, shoveling through my clothes. I packed in such a rush on Friday night that I hardly put any thought into what I was bringing. Now, nearly a week later, I'm suffering the consequences. Looking at what is left in my suitcase, I packed *way* too many pajamas and swimsuits. My go-to jean shorts were drenched in saltwater on Sunday when Cole carried me into the ocean, and now they're downstairs in the laundry room. I wanted to wash them right away, but my mom insisted I wait until I had a full load.

I open the bedroom door and step into the hallway. Cole briefly looks me up and down. "You didn't change."

"The shorts I'm looking for are in the laundry room." I turn, wordlessly asking him to follow me. "They got drenched, remember?"

"You agreed to go in the ocean!" he almost snickers. "Remember?"

He follows me downstairs as I respond. "I did. However, I would've loved to put on a swimsuit first. Apparently, I packed eight of those and only one good pair of shorts."

"Sorry about that." He grimaces.

"Eh, it's okay. It made for a great memory in the end."

"We have a lot of those, don't we?" Cole remarks as we walk into the laundry room.

I reach into the dryer, searching through the slightly wrinkled clothes. I hold up the shorts in the air, seeing the frayed bottoms that I've grown to love. "Got 'em."

As soon as we walk out to the beach, we are invited to join the impromptu cornhole tournament. Cole and I are surely at the very bottom of the team ranking.

I toss the bean bag for what feels like the thirtieth time, and it barely hits the bottom of the board... only to slide off completely. We are playing against McCall and Malik, and it's McCall's turn to throw. I watch with jealousy as the bean bag graciously lands in the hole. Cole's first attempt lands just shy of the board.

"This is rigged!" he jokes as he throws his arms into the air.

"What happened to your axe-cellent aim?" I call out from across the sand.

"Looks like I'm axe-hausted now!" he yells back.

Grandma Rose bursts into laughter on the back patio. "That was a good one!" I watch as she nudges my dad. "These kids have me laughing my axe off."

Wren gasps. "*Grandma!*"

After our game finishes, Cole and I join them on the back patio to watch the tournament unfold. Sierra and Dalton do great, but Eddie and my dad are the clear winners.

After how things ended on Tuesday with a tie between the two houses, Eddie called off the bride vs. groom war for the remainder of the week. In my opinion, deciding to celebrate the families coming together instead of pitting them against one another was the mature choice.

Natalie, Dalton's mother, walks over to us from the Old Lavender House. "Hey!" she cheerily begins. "I was just on my way back from the store and passed some sort of festival in town. They had close to twenty food trucks lined up. It'd be fun to check it out for dinner— my treat. I'm sure we can all find something there!"

At the mere mention of food, my stomach growls. "I'm in!" I exclaim. Everyone else seems to be in agreement as well.

She didn't have to tell us twice. Shortly, we're all climbing into separate vehicles, kids are buckling into car seats, and there's a long train of cars pulling out of the neighboring driveways.

Chapter 31

NO PROMISES

Mrs. Natalie was right about the festival having plenty of food trucks. The trucks line the street, adjacent to the beach. The options seem endless—burgers, tacos, snow cones, barbecue… the list could go on.

Although it's a hard choice to make, Cole and I decide to go the all-American route. We wait in line, place an order, and enter his phone number to receive a text when our burgers are ready. With an estimated ten to fifteen-minute wait, we walk along the path where canopies are set up with a variety of vendors.

There are booths filled with paintings, clay earrings, and a multitude of small gifts like keychains and stickers. In the near distance, a white lighthouse peaks and a local band is performing on the center stage. They're singing a song I've never heard before, yet my head naturally sways to the peaceful melody. Blending into the calm chaos and making a melody of their own is the sound of kids' laughter.

Without yet receiving a text, we head to find a seat, but the picnic tables nearby are all occupied. I plop down in the sand and Cole does the same, sitting beside me.

Looking out at the water, I notice a large group of kids having fun in the sand. I watch as Saylor and Ryder confidently leave my parents' sides to join the other kids that are playing.

"That was us, once upon a time," Cole says, gesturing out to them.

I smile softly and think back to those glorious days. In the summer, we were thankful to have more time to play and roam the neighborhood with our friends. During the school months, we were limited to the short amount of time between homework and an early bedtime.

"Fin?" he begins.

"Yeah?" I turn my attention to him.

"I'm glad you invited me to come. I know it was under weird circumstances, but I've enjoyed this."

"Me too," I say as I notice my mom looking our way and nudging my dad. *How embarrassing.* "I'm pretty positive my mom is enjoying this just as much—if not more than we are. I wouldn't be surprised if she's been sharing updates with your mom about how our relationship is going."

He scoffs. "Oh, *yes*. My mom has asked way too many questions when I've talked to her this week. Similar to your aunt, she wants *all* the details."

"I wouldn't doubt if my mom has been sneaking pictures of us to send to her."

"If she's been stocking up on photos for our future albums, I wouldn't be surprised if my mom has future wedding plans in mind by the time we get back."

My eyes widen slightly. "Whoa! Slow your roll, Dude."

"*Dude?*" Cole gapes. "Dude is practically the most friend-zoned word of them all."

I smile, trying out the same mischievous smirk that Cole has at times. "Who said we were leaving the friend zone?"

"I mean... you were the one to set us up." He pauses. "Well, *basically.*"

I roll my eyes with a smile and turn to watch everything unfold before me. The sun is beginning to set, and it illuminates the festival around us with a golden haze. The tranquil waves that roll in and the slow strum of the band's acoustic guitar make this entire moment ethereal.

I lean back onto my hands, not thinking about the grains of sand that now cover them. "You're right, though," I start. "This week really has been great."

"What happens when it's over?"

Our conversation seems to mirror the one we had just a couple of nights ago at the gazebo. Yet now, it feels different. In a way, it feels more real. The number of days until this trip ends are growing closer by the second, and the two of us have only grown closer as well.

"Well..." I pause, unsure how to respond. "Once we get back home and the clock strikes midnight, we no longer live this fairytale. Everything will be normal."

It has to be normal. I can't allow myself to get attached to the idea of a false future with Cole. Falling down the rabbit hole to an unpredictable Wonderland could end madly. I've experienced firsthand how a relationship can end, and by no means do I want that outcome with Cole. Although, maybe this time it will be different.

Intently, his eyes meet mine. "Our old normal or our new normal?"

I pause and feel as though I'm holding my breath while dancing around eggshells. We're both asking and answering questions without outright saying the words that we mean. "Old?" My tone almost sounds sad and regretful.

"Is that what you want?"

I shrug. Deep down, I think I know the real answer. But I'm far too nervous to admit it to myself, let alone say it aloud. "Maybe?"

"Fin...."

"I don't know, maybe not? No promises. I mean, I *am* enjoying my princess treatment." Graciously, I smile.

"No promises."

Our eye contact doesn't stray—it deepens. A small smile plays on his lips and the motion reaches his eyes. He leans in closer to me. I initially hesitate, then feel myself leaning forward until our faces are less than a foot apart.

I'm confessing more in this moment without speaking than I have allowed myself to physically say. With mere inches between us, my eyes begin to flutter shut. Just as I think my lips are meeting his, a loud screech causes me to jolt up and away from Cole.

I frantically open my eyes just as Saylor launches herself into my lap. "Ryder's going to tag me!" she exclaims.

"It's okay," I reassure her as I nudge her in the opposite direction. "Just tag him back. Go get him, girl!"

Saylor sprints into the crowd of kids. She tags everyone she can, evidently not understanding how the game works.

"I'm sorry," I blurt out to Cole, still reeling over the moment we just shared or... *almost* shared.

He looks slightly flustered. "Yep, yeah. It's okay. No worries." He runs a hand through his brown hair. "We're good, right?"

I nod quickly, bobbing my head up and down. "Yeah, for sure. We're good." The words roll off my tongue before I can think twice. "We're good at being friends and..."

Cole completes the sentence for me. "...And apparently we're a little too good at fake dating?"

I force out a low chuckle. "That too."

We both look out at the horizon as if nothing happened. Truly, *nothing happened*... but if it wasn't for

Saylor and her bad timing, something most certainly could have.

Although, it's for the best that it *didn't*. We'll follow through with our original plans and continue our hoax for the remainder of the week. We'll remain good friends, and everything will surely be fine.

Cole's phone dings. "Our food's ready."

"Good! My stomach is crying out for help."

He extends his hand to help me up and doesn't let go until he grabs our food. We join my family, cramming into the only picnic table that is now available.

The festival is jam-packed with sights that could easily turn my attention elsewhere, yet I can't help but focus on the boy beside me—the boy I came too close to kissing. And what has my head spinning is that it didn't seem like an act. It almost felt too realistic.

I just have to remember that the number one rule in *fake dating* is to keep things *fake*.

FRIDAY
1 Day Until the Wedding

FRIDAY *playlist*

- I Think I'm In Love —————— Kat Dahlia
- Speak Now ——————— Taylor Swift
- Jessie's Girl ——————— Rick Springfield
- Little Lion Man ————— Mumford & Sons
- Sue Me ——————— Sabrina Carpenter
- Watch Your Mouth ——— The Backseat Lovers
- Say You're Sorry ——————— Sara Bareilles
- Set Me Free ——————— Joshua Bassett
- I Did Something Bad ————— Taylor Swift
- Bad Reputation ——— Joan Jett & the Blackhearts
- brutal ——————— Olivia Rodrigo
- Vicious ——————— Sabrina Carpenter
- crashing down ————————— Arlie
- Bruises ————————— Lewis Capaldi
- All Too Well (*10 Minute Version*) (*Taylor's Version*)
  (*From The Vault*) ——————— Taylor Swift
- Solid Ground ———————— Vance Joy
- The Good Ones ————— Gabby Barrett
- Love Come Back To Me ——— Phillip Phillips
- Come Back… Be Here (*Taylor's Version*) ———
  ——————————— Taylor Swift
- Ribs ———————————— Lorde
- Hanging On The Telephone ————— Blondie
- Take Me Home Tonight ——— Eddie Money

Chapter 32

DINER DILEMMA

The four of us are engaged in a lighthearted conversation around our booth at the Sunny Side Diner. By this point, it feels fitting to call it *our* booth. We've become regulars here, and the same waitress with red-rimmed glasses has placed us next to the jukebox without fail.

I slide into the booth and Cole scoots in after me, leaving very little space between us. I've done my best to not make yesterday's close encounter a big deal. Cole must be doing the same because neither of us has mentioned it since.

Our waitress steadily holds a pitcher of water in one hand and a pot of coffee in the other as she refills our glasses. "Can I get anything else for y'all?"

We shake our heads, politely declining. I glance down at her name tag—*Ruby*. With her ruby red glasses, it's fitting.

McCall sighs as she inhales a forkful of scrambled eggs. I give her a concerned glance. "You good?"

"No," she jokes. "I cannot stop thinking about falling on my face tomorrow while walking down the aisle. I'm so not used to walking in heels, even though they aren't that high."

I take a sip of my water. "Don't stress, girl. Sierra said we won't need our heels for the ceremony since we'll be walking in the sand."

McCall sighs. "Oh, that's *such* a relief."

The boys don't look very entertained by our conversation, but I can hear them making jokes under their breath.

Malik cuts in, "Best case scenario is that you fall tonight at the rehearsal dinner instead."

"Great. Now I'm in a dilemma of whether I should be more nervous for tonight or tomorrow."

"Don't worry." I place a reassuring hand on top of hers. "No one remembers what happens at the rehearsal dinner."

Cole chuckles. "Unless McCall falls. Then I'm sure *everyone* will remember." I elbow him under the table. He's wincing when McCall shoots him a look.

"I don't like your boyfriend anymore."

Beside her, Malik is laughing. "Nah, Cole is my new favorite person. I think he's a keeper, Fin."

"I mean, I do like him... as long as he's *not* playing on my nervous weaknesses," she adds.

"I'm just kidding, McCall. *I'm sure you won't fall.* But for other reasons, I think it'll be a rehearsal dinner to remember."

"Agreed. This entire trip has been one to remember." Beneath the table, I feel Cole's hand brush against the side of my leg.

Malik raises his coffee mug. "To a memorable night."

We lift our own drinks, letting the glass and ceramic sides clank together. In unison, we repeat, "To a memorable night."

Chapter 33

LET THE NIGHT BEGIN

In the best way possible, our week has been filled with the hustle and bustle of family gatherings. Yet, we've also had time for solo endeavors, days at the beach, and relaxation. With the rehearsal kicking off soon, it feels surreal. And *wow*, if I'm this excited for Sierra, I can only imagine how she must be feeling.

Now satisfied with my makeup, I spritz the setting spray all over my face and toss my makeup bag back into the suitcase. Making my way down the hall, I knock on Cole's bedroom door. As I'm waiting for him to answer, I take notice of the sign: *Malik, Ryder, & Jesse.* I'm sure it was made way in advance, yet it also serves as a reminder of who could've been here—but who I'm glad is *not*.

The door creaks open. "Hey! Wow," Cole pauses, taking a moment as he finds the right words. "You look amazing."

"Aww, thank you." I glance down timidly at my outfit. I wasn't one hundred percent sure about wearing this sage green jumpsuit, but his reaction makes me feel like this was a good choice. The silver, sparkling heels give me a two-inch boost. My blonde hair is styled half-up, half-down with the top part in a high bun and the bottom flowing in long curls. I wouldn't consider myself an up-and-coming cosmetologist, but I'm pleasantly surprised with how well my hair and makeup turned out tonight.

"You clean up pretty nice yourself, Baxter." His light grey button-up is tucked into dark slacks. His brown, wavy hair looks more defined and sharp, even though there isn't any apparent gel.

"Thanks, Beautiful." He outstretches his hand. "You ready?"

"Absolutely, let's go." I don't even make a face at his use of the nickname. By now, I'm starting to grow accustomed. I take hold of his hand, and he gently squeezes mine. For this to be a motion that we had to practice a few days ago, it feels like second nature now.

Today has been the first day of sporadic weather since we arrived at Sunrise Beach. All week, Aunt Sheryl has been frantically checking the weather app and tracking the ever-changing forecast. Today's outdoor setup has been postponed until first thing tomorrow morning, long before the wedding ceremony begins. Yet tonight, we're cramming the rehearsal dinner plans into this one manor—not that it's really much of a tight squeeze.

Chatter flows through the open downstairs area and extends out to the back patio. An abundance of silver platters line the kitchen counters, filling nearly every square inch. The local catering company set everything up beautifully, and we've all been dying to dig in.

Malik calls out to Cole.

"You go ahead." I nudge him. "I'm going to look for McCall." I let go of his hand as he begins to walk through the sea of people.

Walking outside to this beach view is something that I've grown to love. Even with the looming, overcast skies that are now present, I'm not sure I could ever grow tired of the salt air and wide horizon—even though I may become a tad bit homesick. I've always been surrounded by the lake in Whitefield, but maybe there's hope for me to become just as accustomed to the beach as well. Perhaps I'll spend the rest of my life going back and forth between saltwater and fresh. It sounds like the best of both worlds.

I spot McCall at the end of the patio with an empty chair beside her. Walking over, I claim the seat as my own. The flowy, blush pink dress she's wearing brings out the color in her face and makes her high, defined cheekbones even more prominent. Her dark brown hair is straight, just barely brushing the top of her shoulders and puff sleeves.

It's almost weird to see everyone all dressed up for an event like this, rather than a game of baseball or a relay race.

Wren walks up to us, practically beaming from ear to ear. "Hey! Have either of you seen Kyle?"

I scan the area, looking for Dalton's younger brother. "No, I haven't. Everything okay?"

"Yeah, I just…" Wren's words trail off and are replaced with a blushing smile.

"Wren!" I gasp. "Do you li—"

"Shh!" She instantaneously clasps her hand over my mouth. "I don't want to hear anything from you, okay? You're dating our neighbor for crying out loud."

"*Ouch*," McCall giggles. "She's coming for your relationship now."

"And?" I shrug nonchalantly. "Cole's cute."

Wren grimaces. "*Ew*, Finley."

Sensing that it's slightly bothering her, I continue in the typical older sister fashion. "I mean you and Kyle *would* make a cute couple. He's your first crush and—"

"Gross! Would you stop it? I'm going to find him myself."

"Go get 'em, little sis!" After a moment I chime in, "But, wait a few years!"

"Y'all are such a hot mess." McCall chuckles. "I couldn't imagine you as my older sister navigating me through relationships at that age."

"Oh, I'm sure I'll be *wonderful* at it." I'm already stirring up a few plans in my head.

"Poor Wren."

Wren is fifteen—the same age I was when Jesse and I started dating. I remember feeling so mature at that age… other than when my mom tagged along on all of our dates. She accompanied us until Jesse turned sixteen and started driving. On our first movie date, my mom sat two rows behind us, chomping on popcorn and *loudly* slurping the last drop of her soda. I can still vividly picture the embarrassment marked on my face, hardly believing that she would dare to do such a thing while I was on a *date*.

Yet now, watching Wren and Kyle, I know I will most likely sneak into her first date as well—and her second. I may need to dress fully incognito and watch from afar. Better yet, if she ever goes out with Kyle, I'm nearly positive that Sierra will sneak in with me. After all, he will soon be her fifteen-year-old brother-in-law.

Perfectly on time with my inner monologue, Sierra struts over. In her short, white dress, she looks blissfully relieved to see me. She grabs a chair and slides it toward us, making herself comfortable. "I have kind of a weird question for you about the rehearsal. Dalton and I have already done a brief run-through, and it's pretty simple, but we would really like to be certain of the entire wedding party's placement. I just really want it to be perfect."

Slowly, I nod as I try to figure out what she's implying. "Okay. Where do I come in?"

"You... *and* Cole. Would you mind standing in for us?"

"I'd be the bride and Cole, the groom?"

"Yes, exactly!"

If I've learned one thing from watching my share of reality TV, it's that you should *always* give the bride what she wants, even if it causes discomfort. I'd do anything to give her the perfect ceremony, and I truthfully don't mind standing in for her in the slightest.

"I'm in! It honestly sounds kind of fun."

"Great! Tomorrow you'll be walking with Logan, but his flight has been delayed until the morning, so this works out perfectly!"

"Sounds like a plan."

Sierra beams. "I'll go grab your groom!"

Chapter 34

THE STAND-INS

As I make my way to the edge of the staircase, Eddie meets me with an extended elbow. Playing my role as the bride's stand-in, I instinctively smile as I lace my arm through his. We reach the bottom of the steps, and the sand is cool beneath my toes.

As I walk down the aisle, I keep a fixated gaze on one person. In this moment, Cole is my groom—my fictitious happily ever after. *Oh, the irony.*

Eddie plays his part and quickly 'gives me away', but I'm sure he'll be emotional during tomorrow's ceremony. For someone who seems like such a tough guy, he's genuinely a teddy bear with the biggest soft spot for his daughter. Sierra's real-life *'Eddie-Bear'*.

Cole smiles as I reach him. "Hi, Babe," he whispers.

"Hey, *Lover Boy*."

Cole envelops my hands in his. Ryder volunteered to fill in for the officiant tonight. I look down at my little brother and notice the sheet of paper he's holding. It is covered in my mother's handwriting.

"Welcome family and friends! We are gathered here today to celebrate Sierra and Dalton. This is not the beginning of a new relationship, but it is the start of a new chapter in their lives together. Blah, blah, blah...." He turns his attention to me. "Do you, Finley—*Sierra*," he corrects, "take Cole—*Dalton*, to be your lawfully wedded husband?"

"I do." I can feel the blush rising in my cheeks.

Ryder glances back down at his wrinkled sheet of paper before looking at Cole. This time, he skips over the names. "Do you take her to be your lawfully wedded wife?"

Cole's eyes never falter on mine as he recites, "I do."

"You may now kiss the bride."

Neither Cole nor myself move. How many people are watching us? Twenty to thirty? Possibly more? All the bridesmaids and groomsmen are behind us, watching intently. Family members watch from afar while some, such as Eddie and Aunt Sheryl, have a front-row seat.

Without a word being said, Cole and I recognize one another's thoughts of '*What do we do?*'. This is far beyond my preparations for being a stand-in bride. I only agreed to help Sierra map out the rehearsal. I shouldn't be taking the spotlight on her white veil occasion. Surely, someone will speak now and let us know that our roles as the stand-ins are complete. Yet, of course, all eyes stay on Cole and me.

"What are you waiting for?" Ryder makes a face. "Just kiss already!"

I can hear my heartbeat in my chest, drowning out everything around me. It seems there's only one thing to do. In these few seconds that feel like days, I let my mind go back to last night. I let myself think about what *almost* happened.

The space between us grows smaller and smaller. With my hands still woven in his, I take a step toward him. As I feel my eyes flutter shut, I prepare to close the space between us. Our noses brush against one another. Simultaneously, a loud, worrisome gasp echoes from behind me.

I spin on my heels, seeing Peyton frozen in place with one hand clasped over her mouth and the other holding the bottom of her belly.

Matt rushes to her side, frantic. "Peyton, what's wrong?"

"My water just broke. I'm going into *labor*."

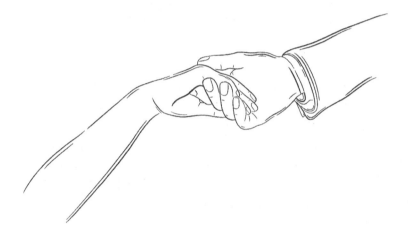

Chapter 35

CHAOS RETURNING

As I'm standing frozen at the altar, the chaos begins. Peyton does her best to hurry to the car, only her stride is nothing more than a slow waddle. Matt is right behind her, his face as white as Ryder's sheet of paper. Blaire and Caroline rush inside to grab their shoes and phones. Sierra offers to grab extra clothes for them, but Peyton assures her that her hospital bag is waiting in the car.

"I'm so sorry, Sierra. I was really hoping the baby would wait until after the wedding. I'm sad that I won't get to witness your big day."

"Are you kidding? You have every reason to be happy! We're all so excited for you. If you're up for it, I'll have someone video chat with you during the wedding. You won't miss a thing."

"I'd love that! I wouldn't want to miss it for the world."

Grandma Rose reassures Matt that Juniper will be well taken care of. "Don't you worry about this one. We have a village here to watch over her."

After giving Juniper a tight hug and a kiss on her forehead, he makes a mad dash to the car. He is practically spinning tires as they back out of the driveway.

After *that* chaos has finally settled, the normal chaos is returning to Hollow Oak. It didn't take long for Juniper to begin to cry for her parents or for Grandma Rose to immediately spring into peek-a-boo, knowing that it is her favorite game. Her tears are quickly replaced with a cheerful baby giggle. Malik is expressively pretending to throw a football mid-conversation with my dad and Uncle Malcolm. Snacking on the wide selection of food, Wren and I catch up. In between bites of hors d'oeuvres, I try to slyly bring up Kyle, but she immediately shoots the topic down.

Against the sea of faces and voices, Cole is nowhere to be found. I try to pinpoint the last place I saw him, but when the pandemonium ensued, he was lost in the crowd.

Oh goodness, did I seriously leave him at the altar? My mind wanders, once again replaying the gap between us that was on the verge of closing. *Again.*

Yet now, as I lean against the doorframe of the back patio, it's all I can think about—everything that didn't happen… and everything that I wish *would have.*

I feel as though there's so much left unsaid between us. I have so much more to say now than ever before.

We've had one of the best weeks here—one of our best weeks *together*. And although it's slightly terrifying that he may not feel the same way, I can't shake the urge to explain myself to him. I need to explain the thoughts that are rushing through my head like one million glimmering comets.

Because at least for me... everything that was supposed to be fake has never felt more real.

I further observe the room, still not spotting him in the mix of scattered crowds. Once the bright sky faded to black, everyone gathered inside and began sharing embarrassing stories of Sierra and Dalton. While their history is entertaining, my mind ponders over Cole and our future.

I slide the large glass door to the side and step through. The party's chatter dies down as I close the door behind me. On the off chance that Cole's outside, I go searching for him. From the back patio, I don't see him.

Where is he? I silently wonder.

I'm about to head back inside and check upstairs when I hear a faint rustling to my right. I decide to follow the sound in the sand, so I crouch down to take off my heels. As my blonde hair swoops in front of my face and my hands undo the clasp, I hear a voice ring out from the backside of the house.

"Finley?"

I freeze. I immediately recognize the voice, but it belongs to someone who I truly, wholeheartedly hope is *not here* of all places. Maybe it's all in my head.

Yet, after I don't respond, the voice calls out again. It's even louder this time and gives me no reason to believe that it's a figment of my imagination. "Finley? Is that you?"

I kick off my heels and begrudgingly stand to face... *him.*

Jesse.

Chapter 36

THE ANTAGONIST

"*Jesse.*" Saying his name aloud solidifies that he actually had the nerve to show up here. "What are you *doing*?" I hiss.

I fear that anyone inside will see him through the glass doors. The last thing I need is questions about my ex. I briskly walk onto the beach in hopes that Jesse will follow me.

Thankfully, he does so, nearly tracing my exact steps. Jesse blurts out, "I need to explain myself."

I abruptly turn to face him. "I don't need your explanation, nor do I care to hear it. I don't know what made you think it's okay to just show up here… but you need to leave."

"Finley, you're the best thing that's ever happened to me." Jesse takes a step closer to me, now way too close for my comfort. I inch backward, putting more space between us.

"*Seriously?*" My voice rises. "Yet you still *cheated on me?*"

"Stop," he scolds with his jaw clenched. "If you would just listen to me—"

"No, Jesse! *You* listen." I can feel the intense pressure rising in my chest as I take another step away from him. "You don't get to just pop back into my life and try to change things!"

"Cheating on you was my *biggest* mistake, Finley!"

"I'm over you and your mistakes!" I shout back. "You never learned from *any* of them!" I storm off, getting closer to the water.

"*No.*" He sternly points a finger at me. "You're *not* going to do that!"

"Tell me exactly what it is that I'm *not* going to do!"

"You're not going to blame me for everything." My mouth drops. "*Please,*" I scoff.

"Cheating on you was my *only* mistake. I was a great boyfriend."

"Oh, get over yourself! *Everyone* makes mistakes, Jesse! *I* made mistakes in our relationship, and you certainly did too."

He crosses his arms like a toddler who didn't get his way. "Fine, name one."

"Sure thing!" I expressively throw my arms in the air. "You didn't listen to me. You may have heard what I was saying, but I think you were too self-absorbed to ever truly *listen.* Everything was always about you."

Even with the distant lights that barely shine on us, I can still see Jesse rolling his eyes.

"I practically gave up my friends to hang out with yours. You didn't even know the people who had been close to me—"

"Like Cole?" he interrupts.

I narrow my eyes. *"Don't* go there. Cole has absolutely nothing to do with any of this."

"I mean, undeniably you and Cole were always *close.* Looks like the two of you are even closer now. You certainly didn't give *him* up."

I furrow my brows. "Did you seriously drive all the way here just to whine about *Cole?*"

"It just had to be him, didn't it?"

Wordlessly, I shake my head. I cannot believe I'm having this conversation right now. Despite my efforts to stay headstrong, I'm beginning to acknowledge the uneasiness in my stomach and the shaky rise and fall of my breath.

Jesse blows out a huff of air. "Don't act clueless. You broke up with me, and then you brought him here? I'm just expected to believe that all of it is… what? A random coincidence?"

"I don't care what you believe. Anything that happens between Cole and me has nothing to do with you!" I shout back. I shut my eyes and take a deep breath. This conversation is exhausting. *Jesse is exhausting.* My thoughts are flooded with bad memories of the past—our argument at the drive-in, the screaming match on our drive home on New Year's Eve, and Valentine's Day when I saw him making out with another girl. Squeezing my eyes shut even tighter now, I wish this moment could just go away.

A new voice adds to the mix. "What's going on here?" I open my eyes and see Cole walking over from my left.

A sigh of relief escapes me just before Jesse is set off once again. "Well, if it isn't the man of the hour!"

The panic must show on my face because Cole plants himself in front of me like a shield. "I'm sorry," I mouth to him.

"What are you doing here?" he asks Jesse.

"*Me?*" Jesse acts dumbfounded. "What are *you* doing? Filling in as Finley's rebound?"

I roll my eyes. "You sound like a psychopath."

He stares directly at Cole. "I should've known it was going to be you." Having to look around Cole, he gives me a glare. "That was the plan all along, huh?" With every word, his voice gets louder—*angrier.*

"You need to calm down, man." Cole attempts to take control of the situation.

Glancing at the glass door, I see fragments of the party pass in a blur. "Jesse, you need to go. I should be celebrating my cousin and her fiancé right now, not bandaging your bruised ego. You need to leave."

He looks distant as if he hasn't heard anything I said. Although I've seen him mad before, I've never seen him quite like *this*.

Cole takes a commanding step in his direction. "She asked you to leave."

"I should've known you'd be the one to take her from me," Jesse lashes out.

Clearly over this never-ending conversation, Cole doesn't hold back. "Look! No one took anything from you, but if you want to blame someone, blame yourself. Hold *yourself* accountable for the idiotic choices you made when the two of you were together! Finley deserves *so* much more than the awful way you treated her! I mean seriously, you cheated on—"

Swiftly, Jesse closes the gap between them as his fist makes contact with the bottom of Cole's jaw.

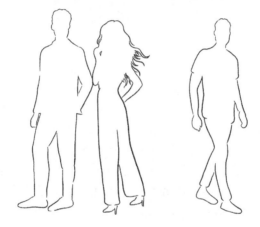

Chapter 37

LET IT ALL OUT

Cole immediately hits the sand with a *thud*.

"Cole!" I yell as I drop to my knees beside him. He lifts his head and begins to stand. Before he can say anything, I rise with every ounce of fury built up inside me. I strut over to Jesse and grab a fistful of his shirt. "*You* ruined our relationship on your own. Cole and I have nothing to do with your myriad of mistakes."

"Fin—"

"No! I'm *done*, Jesse! There's no more *Finley-this* or *Finley-that*. It's over! I don't want to see you around my family, and an instance like this will *never* happen again."

Slowly, like he's finally putting the puzzle pieces together, he nods.

"You're leaving." I let go of his shirt and shove him away from me.

In utter silence, he walks away. I watch as his silhouette disappears around the corner of the house, and then I hear the all-too-familiar sound of his truck.

Cole winces, reaching a hand up to the spot where Jesse sucker-punched him. With only the light of the moon, I notice that the skin tone of his jaw is already becoming a darker shade.

"You're my knight in shining armor," he jokes.

"No, that's all you. You showed up just in time. Stay here," I tell him. "I'm going to get you some ice."

Darting inside, I head straight for the freezer. I've barely made it into the kitchen when McCall grabs my forearm and pulls me aside. *"What the heck* just happened?"

"It's a long story, but I'll explain everything tonight. Please tell me no one else saw."

"No, I had just walked to the back door since I hadn't seen you in a while. Then I saw… well, I don't know what exactly I saw. I just know that it didn't look good."

Leaving the hustle and bustle of the rehearsal dinner once again, I rush back outside to Cole.

"I could've taken him," he says as I hand over the icepack. Cautiously, he lifts it up to his face.

I plop down beside him in the sand, pull my knees to my chest, and let out a defeated sigh.

Trying to crack jokes, Cole continues. "I mean, I didn't think he would actually *punch* me. I just needed some time to prepare, you know?" He chuckles lowly. "I sure didn't get the warning before his low blow."

Despite his efforts to make this a lighthearted moment, I can't even force out a smile. Instead, I warily place my head in my hands.

"Hey, it's okay," Cole reassures, understanding my current emotional state. He scoots closer and wraps an arm around me.

For reasons other than the slight chill outside and the warmth he brings, I'm grateful for his embrace. I'm grateful for *him*.

"It's okay, Fin," he says. "I'm okay, just a little banged up."

With the image replaying of Jesse swinging at him and the screaming match with me, my voice begins to waiver. "It should've never happened, though. He shouldn't have been here."

He nods in agreement.

I lean closer until my head is resting on his shoulder. I just need a moment to cool down. Cole's steady and solid ground feels like a breath of fresh air. As I watch the waves crash onto the shore, I let my thoughts spill out. "I thought I was over it," my words crack. "I'm certainly over *him,* but everything that's happened with him is hard to forget." I gently shake my head. "I feel like it's tattooed on my brain, possibly ruining every future relationship."

"That makes sense," he replies.

I lift my head up to face him. "I'm almost worried that for every happy memory I make, there are two bad ones waiting around the corner. In the beginning, my relationship with Jesse was good. In the end, it was awful. What if every relationship is like that? Just temporary happiness?"

"I promise it's not just temporary."

Genuinely, I ask, "How do you know?"

"Because relationships take work, trust, and communication. If you ask me, Jesse lacks multiple of those things. Plus, good people are out there."

"Like you?" I nudge his side and crack a smile.

Cole chuckles. "I mean *I* wasn't going to brag on myself, but now that you've mentioned it...."

I laugh, even though I silently agree. It's not hard to see that Cole is *one of the good ones.*

Continuing to mention all the right things, he says, "It takes time to get through the full healing process. You don't have to forgive or forget in order to move past it. Unfortunately, just because you move on, it doesn't mean you're going to forget everything that happened. The good and the bad, it sticks with you."

I nod slowly, wondering to myself what I did to deserve such a good friend.

"But just because something sticks with you, doesn't mean it's always going to break you."

"Thanks for the love advice, Romeo."

"I knew you'd come around on the nicknames."

"Oh, definitely not. I'm just giving you a taste of your own medicine."

Still holding the ice pack onto his jaw, he winces. "Speaking of medicine, I may need some," he jokes. "Nah, I'm just kidding. I'm fine, really."

If only for a moment, I almost forgot everything that happened. "Ugh, he's such a jerk. I know I agreed to be in a relationship with him, but it still feels like he used me somehow," I finish.

Cole sighs. "Believe me, I know the feeling well."

"What do you mean?" I've hardly finished my question when his phone begins to ring.

He grabs it from his pocket and rises to his feet. "I should take this. I'll be right back."

Now sitting alone, I urge myself to think about anything other than tonight's fiasco. Foolishly enough, the first thing that comes to mind is my makeup. From my tears trying to escape earlier, I'm sure it looks rough now. I get Cole's attention and silently motion that I'm heading inside.

I walk through the crowds, heading to the upstairs bathroom. On my way, Saylor questions if I've seen Ryder. I have not, but she urges me to help search anyways. I'm coaxed into a quick game of hide-and-seek, finding him hidden behind a curtain. I'm finally able to escape to the bathroom. Just as I was expecting, some of my eye makeup is smudged. I take a moment to freshen up my face and comb through my hair before heading outside.

Once I reach the cool sand, Cole is nowhere in sight. I shout out his name a few times but get no response. Instead of him, I'm met with McCall walking to my side.

"Hey, have you seen Cole?" I question.

248

Her wide eyes sink, going soft. "He went *home*, Finley."

Chapter 38

FAKING IT

"*What?*" I manage to ask, nearly breathless once again tonight.

"He didn't say much," McCall explains with a worried glance. "He only said that he needed to leave. He asked if I would let you know, but then he rushed out the front door."

Even though it makes no sense, I slowly nod. Somehow, Cole unexpectedly leaving with no explanation feels so much worse than the drama from earlier tonight.

I don't care what Jesse thinks of me. But Cole? I care way more than I've ever allowed myself to believe. I can't lose him like this.

My mind races, trying to find a solution. Better yet, I'm searching for the *reason* Cole left. Maybe tonight was too much for him. Maybe *I* was. Jesse coming here and Cole getting punched… it all happened because of me. I was the bridge between the two of them. I'm the *reason*.

I think back to the last thing he said before his phone rang. When I mentioned how I felt used by Jesse, Cole expressed that he knew the feeling well. *Was that because of me too?* Surely, it is. Just a few days ago, I sprung the idea of fake dating on him so that I wasn't alone. To benefit myself, I brought him here and had him play along all week. Like a puppet on a string, he participated in my family's games. Day after day, he held my hand. Maybe I *had* used him.

"Are you okay?" McCall's words jerk me back to reality.

"Yeah, yeah. I'll be fine," I murmur.

"Can you tell me what happened?"

I glance around the room and see all the familiar faces that are within earshot. "Later," I promise. "We need to get through this first."

Understanding, she nods. "Okay, as long as you don't need to get anything off your chest now."

I dab under my eyes and put up the best front I can muster. "Oh, there's *plenty* of things I need to get off my chest. The problem is, we don't have the time."

McCall's eyes go wide. "*That* much happened tonight?"

"Eh, not exactly…." I say through gritted teeth. "This story goes back at least four months."

"*What?* Oh my goodness!" Her words nearly echo through the foyer.

"Shh," I say in a hurry before she can loudly ask any more questions. "Will you please keep me company? I desperately need a distraction."

The thought of Cole not being here makes my eyes sting, but the thought of how much is still left unsaid nearly starts the waterworks.

Finding my first distraction, I walk over to the food and pile some onto a plate. McCall stands beside me, whispering, "You were seemingly just on the verge of tears. Are you sure you're okay?"

I turn to her, forcing a smile. "Sometimes, you just have to fake *it till you make it.*" *I've gotten pretty good at that.*

We join the rest of the crew, making small talk. Conversations strike up about the excitement of the wedding and updates on Peyton's labor. The baby should be here by the morning, if not sooner.

As I walk through the house, laugh at one of Ryder's jokes, and smile at the stories my family tells… *I fake it.* But with the knot of dread that sits in my stomach… I don't feel like I'm going *to make it.*

McCall has done a great job of staying by my side. She's done so well that I've yet to have five seconds to myself. As she's joking around with Blaire, I use this moment to quickly sneak upstairs.

I move around my room, searching for my phone. Maybe Cole has called or texted, and I've been too distracted to have thought of this possibility sooner. Maybe this entire instance has been one big misunderstanding.

I manage to find my phone, but once I pick it up, I notice the screen stays black. Of course, my battery is drained to a lovely zero percent. I plug it in and wait on the edge of the bed, anxiously bouncing my leg up and down. After what feels like forever, the screen lights up. A glimmer of hope lights up inside of me as well.

I scroll through the list of notifications on my phone, and not a single one is from Cole. Double-checking, I scroll through them once more. Still... *nothing*. I tap a series of buttons, trying to call him.

I'm met with his voicemail on the other line.

Although, one of us may not have a good signal. After all, we haven't had much luck in this small town. Even when we were stranded the other day, our phones were useless. I take this thought and run with it— literally. I unplug my phone and rush outside to the second-story balcony. I descend the stairs, trying to call him once more. With the ringing of my phone now echoing in my ear, I faintly hear something in the distance.

Going to inspect further, I hurry in the direction of the sound and wince as the rocks dig into my bare feet. Even so, my glimmer of hope grows with each step. One step, two steps, *three*. By the fourth, my hope comes to a screeching halt and is replaced with worry.

The sound isn't coming from Cole but rather from his phone.

It's laying face-up in the middle of the driveway. The photo displayed is the one McCall took of us at the

Sunny Side Diner. I'm leaning into him and looking a whole lot happier than I feel at this current moment.

Bending down, I begrudgingly pick up his phone and decline my own call. A single notification is on the screen. It reads,

YOUR MESSAGE TO 'FIN   ' FAILED TO SEND.

Chapter 39

THERE

Back home, I used to look out my bedroom window, and it just so happened to perfectly line up with Cole's. In a weird way, knowing that he was only a few yards away became one of my greatest comforts growing up.

Seventh-grade math was rough, yet Cole was there for me during my dramatic afternoons.

When I terribly lost a game of childhood tag, Cole was there. Even as the daily games of tag came to a close, our time together never faltered.

As my breakup was fresh, he was there. On day three of me sulking in bed, Cole entered my room and persuaded me to leave the house. We went to Bertha's where—with an absurdly large ice cream cone in my hand—I let out the last of the tears I shed over Jesse.

But now? He's not here. He's not here to help me through this, and he's not here when I need his words of wisdom.

As I look out my bedroom window at Hollow Oak, it's the opposite of comfort—even though it has thus been the epitome of comfort this week. I see the waves crashing, hitting hard against one another. I see the sand where he landed after getting punched.

I see the lack of him around me.

Yet possibly even more, I feel the gnawing sense of worry over what made him leave so suddenly. Was it me, or was it something else? What sent him leaving Sunrise Beach within a matter of minutes?

Chapter 40

NOT ALL ENDINGS

Deciding to call it an early night, I turn away from the depressing windowsill. No longer up for socialization, I change into a comfortable pair of navy blue sweatpants and a soft white tee. Using a wipe, I scrub away all remnants of my makeup. I untwist the bun that held the top half of my hair and let the wild curls flow. Very similar to the thoughts that are racing through my mind—it's a mess.

As I'm nearly giving in to the urge of sleep while sitting cross-legged on my bed, McCall bursts through our door. "There you are!" she exclaims. Judging by the way her expression shifts, she must notice how exhausted I look. "Oh, Fin," she whispers.

Wordlessly, she climbs onto the bed and envelops me in a tight hug. Without saying a word, I begin to cry. Not small sniffles but full-out sobs—and I hate every second of it.

Weirdly enough, I mourn.

I mourn a lot of things, finally allowing myself to close the door on my past. Although, as I'm locking that door, I wonder about the one that never had the full chance to open—*the door that leads to Cole.* I mourn what could've been, along with what I fear will now never be, thanks to my ex and his hash decisions. Better yet, *thanks to me.*

I explain everything to McCall. *Everything.*

From the breaking points in my relationship with Jesse to the cheating, I tell her all of it. I dive into the details about my spontaneous idea of fake dating Cole, as well as every emotion I've had throughout the experience. In-depth, I explain the fight that happened just hours ago and share with her every word that I can remember.

"Finley…" she cautiously begins. "Can I tell you what I think?"

"*Please* do," I exasperate. "You're the first person I've told any of this. I'm in serious need of advice and girl talk."

Thinking, she pauses for a moment and pulls her knees to her chest. "After everything that's happened between you and Cole, do you *honestly* think he would leave without a good reason?"

"My ex-boyfriend drove out of his way to start a fight with Cole because of our relationship. And it's not even a *real* relationship! I'd say that's a pretty good reason to just up and leave."

"I don't know. I'm not sure why he left, but I don't think the fight with Jesse had anything to do with it."

"But surely after I—"

She cuts me off before I can get another word out. "I've seen the way he looks at you—even when you're not looking. I think you could be a part of something much worse, and he would still hang the moon for you."

"That may be a little dramatic," I say with a glimmer of a smile.

"Okay, but still," McCall chuckles. "Just think about it."

Those thoughts bring back a montage of my favorite moments from this week: the thought-out date on the boardwalk with flowers surrounding us, slow dancing terribly in the deserted Sunny Side Diner, and stealing the last slice of pizza and sprinting out to the gazebo. In nearly all of those moments, it was just the two of us. There was no real need for us to pretend.

McCall says, "I don't think you're allowing yourself to imagine the possibility of a happy ending."

I listen intently as she carries on.

"It's almost as if you're trying to convince yourself that your *real* feelings about Cole are fake. You're reading so far between the lines, you can't even see that he has those same feelings for you. Not all relationships are bad, and not all boys are Jesse! Some take the punches instead of throwing them." She winks.

"You know that not all endings are happy, but not all endings are sad, either."

"I can't lose him, McCall. I don't think I ever realized how much of a role he's played in my life until now. I've taken him for granted for too long. And maybe... maybe it wasn't *all* fake."

"It's about time you admitted it out loud! I'm telling you, I don't think it was all fake for him, either."

I sit in silence, unsure of how to respond.

"The two of you had me fooled all along." She lifts a finger. "*That's* impressive."

I chuckle.

"So... what are you doing *here*?"

"Um... talking to you."

"That's exactly the issue," she notes. "You need to talk to Cole. Call him until he picks up."

"About that...." I lift his phone into the air. "This was in the driveway."

McCall gasps. "I swear you two are living in a fairytale. This is like a Cinderella story! You could always drive back to Whitefield tonight after your Prince Charming."

I shake my head with a smirk. "I don't even have a car, nonetheless a pumpkin. Plus, tomorrow is the wedding."

"I'll cover for you and help you with a car. My dad's keys have been hanging on the hook all week."

Laughing, I say, "That's insane. There's *no way* I'm taking your dad's car! And there's no way either of us could pull that off. With no disrespect, you're absolutely the worst liar I know."

"I'll step up my act tomorrow. After watching you and Cole fool us all, I think I have this one covered."

I shake my head. "No, I can't do that. I can't just steal a car and sneak away."

I jolt awake. The room is pitch black, aside from the alarm clock that displays *1:37 AM* in bright red. My mind is foggy, unable to remember the nightmare that wakes me. Then, it all comes rushing back to me.

What makes it worse is that it's not at all fictitious. Panicked, I shake McCall awake. After hours of talking, we both drifted off in my bed.

"McCall!" I hiss.

Groggily, her eyes partially open.

"I forgot it! I forgot my bridesmaid dress at home!"

Half asleep, her words jumble together in a verbal brain dump. "I mean… I *guess* that works for a cover story." She rolls over. "But I thought you decided against going back."

"It's not a cover story, McCall! I seriously forgot my dress."

SATURDAY
The Day of the Wedding

SATURDAY *playlist*

- Getaway Car ———————— Taylor Swift
- Home To You ————————— Jack Botts
- All I Want —————————— Kodaline
- For Your Love ———————— GUNNAR
- Beginning Middle End ————— Leah Nobel
- Death By A Thousand Cuts ———— Taylor Swift
- Lay It On Me —————————— Vance Joy
- For Real This Time ————— Gracie Abrams
- Talk Too Much ————————— COIN
- Kiss Her You Fool —————— Kids That Fly
- Something That I Want ———— Grace Potter
- Never Felt A Love Like This ——————
  ——————— Galantis, Hook N Sling, Dotan
- long story short —————— Taylor Swift
- Missing Piece ———————— Vance Joy
- Enchanted ————————— Taylor Swift
- Someone To You-Acoustic ——— BANNERS
- I See the Light —— Mandy Moore, Zachary Levi
- Today Was A Fairytale (Taylor's Version) ———
  ——————————————— Taylor Swift

Chapter 41

THE GETAWAY CAR

In a little over twelve hours, I'm supposed to be walking down the aisle as a bridesmaid... and I'm missing the one thing I need. In my rushed attempt to pack, the dress must've slipped my mind, and I haven't realized it was missing until now—the day of the wedding.

Doing my best to not wake anyone at two in the morning, I tiptoe down the long hallway and creak open my parent's bedroom door. As I'm making my way to the bed, I walk straight into the footboard and stub my toe—*hard. Ow, ow, ow!* I practically scream the words in my head.

Nudging her, I whisper, "Mom? Mom?"

Nothing. She doesn't even move the slightest bit.

"Mom," I say, louder this time. "I forgot my bridesmaid dress at home. I need to take your car to go pick it up."

Still... *nothing.*

Gently, I shake her, remembering that she's the deepest sleeper in the world. My dad rolls over. "I forgot my dress. Is it okay if I take your car?" All I get in response is a loud snore.

"Mm-hmm," my mom finally groans.

"Where are your keys?" With no response yet again, she's clearly fallen back asleep. "Are your keys in your purse?" I try again.

"Hmm."

I walk over to the nightstand and begin to dig through the contents of her bag—Tylenol, receipts, her wallet, cough drops... yet *no car keys.* I run my hand over the top of the nightstand and dresser, checking both to see if the keys are lying on top. A pair of my dad's jeans are draped over the chair in the corner, so I check his pockets next. No luck.

I give up, now quietly scurrying back down the hallway to my room.

McCall is sitting on the edge of her bed when I walk in. "So?" she presses. "What did she say?"

I plop onto my bed, defeated. "Nothing, she's passed out. I looked everywhere for her keys, but I couldn't find them. I have no clue where else to look."

"*Well...*" she cautions in a sing-song tone.

"What?"

"I have a backup plan in mind."

"No. No, McCall. There's *no way* I'm taking your dad's car!"

"If you don't, then I will. I don't condone

stealing by any means, but we have no other choice! If we wait any longer, we'll have to break the news to Aunt Sheryl that you forgot your dress—and that will *not* be a positive start to the big day. Aunt Sheryl rises before the sun, you know."

I nod slowly. "With an hour-and-a-half drive to Whitefield, that puts us getting back at five if we leave *right now*. The last thing we need is for anyone to realize that we're missing with your dad's prized possession."

"So, you're cool with taking the car?"

I grimace. "Well *no*… but what other option do we have? I can't wake anyone else up to beg for a ride. Because of that, I guess I'm in. But—" I lift a finger. "I'm not getting behind the wheel."

"No worries, I'll drive."

"Have you ever driven that car before?"

She waves a hand. "There's no time for logistics right now. It's time for the first step of our plan: *The Getaway*."

As she leaps out of bed, I plant my palm on my forehead. I don't know what's gotten into McCall this early in the morning, and I certainly don't know how well this 'plan' is going to blow over. Still in my pajamas, I slide on the bunny slippers that Saylor gifted me for Christmas and follow her lead.

Walking down the hall, she stops at the door with the sign that reads, *Malik, Ryder, & Jesse*. The sight of Jesse's name makes me cringe, and knowing that Cole isn't behind the door nearly makes me sick with worry. The unknown is far too wide.

McCall taps her finger on the sign, pointing out Malik's name. Quiet as a mouse, she whispers, "Step one." Tip-toeing inside, I shut the door behind us as she shakes him awake.

Unlike my mom, Malik wakes in an instant. Ryder stays passed out two beds over. I try not to focus on the empty bed in the middle. It's dark in the room, yet I notice that most of Cole's belongings are still here. That alone gives me the smallest inkling of hope.

"We need your help," McCall says to Malik.

Groggily, he sits up on his elbows. "What do you need help with in the middle of the night? Robbing a store?"

"Eh, you're not far off. We need to steal—"

"*Temporarily borrow*," I correct.

"Right. We need to *temporarily borrow* Dad's car."

"*Ha!*" Malik calls out. "You two can have fun with that, but there's no way I'm getting involved in your heist. I'm going back to sleep."

"Malik, *please*," she begs. "We just need your help getting the car to the bottom of the driveway. If we start it where it is now, it'll be loud enough to wake Dad up. And if it does, then I'll be sure to tell him about the flat tire we got on Monday."

"Look," I start, crouching down beside Malik. "I hate this idea even more than you do—and it feels important to note that it was *not* my idea—but I don't know what else to do. I forgot my bridesmaid dress at home, and that's why McCall and I need to leave right away. I can't find my parents' keys, and I feel like this is our only option."

Malik groans. "I can't believe I'm agreeing to this *awful* plan, but if anything goes south, I had nothing to do with it."

"Yeah, yeah. I gotcha," McCall expresses. "Just help us get the car to the bottom of the driveway. I'm going to grab Dad's keys. Y'all meet me outside."

"Okay," he agrees.

I face him, adding, "We'll need you to cover for us as well. If anyone asks, we're still sound asleep in bed. Try not to let anyone outside before we get back. Call and let us know if we're at risk of getting caught."

Crawling out of bed, he looks me up and down as though I've lost my mind. "You're asking an awful lot for someone wearing bunny slippers."

"Okay, it's in neutral," McCall expresses from behind the wheel. "You can start pushing!"

It takes a good bit of effort for us to get the car rolling in the gravel, but it gradually gets easier as we're going downhill. It's now past 2 AM, and the dark sky proves that the three of us should still be sleeping. We most certainly should not be staging a rescue mission.

Once we're halfway down the driveway and don't have to exert as much energy to push the car, Malik asks, "What happened to Cole?"

I shrug. "You're guess is as good as mine. I only know that he went back to Whitefield and that he dropped his phone on his way out. I found it in the driveway last night."

"Ah, so that's why you're hijacking a car. To get your dress... and to see him."

"Borrowing," I correct. "And the car was your sister's idea." I don't confirm nor deny his suspicion about Cole.

We reach the golden gates that precede Hollow Oak. "Alright, this should be far enough. No one should really be able to hear this far out. You'll just sound like another car on the main road."

"Thanks, Malik. I owe you one," McCall says.

"You definitely do, especially since you blackmailed me into helping." He shoots her a look.

McCall pats her hand on the passenger seat. "You ready to be my accomplice?"

"Please stop making this sound like a real crime."

"Not a real crime, *just a little joy ride in the getaway car.*"

Chapter 42

THE RESCUE MISSION

The drive back to my hometown consists of nearly abandoned roads, foggy and dark skies, and racing against the clock.

I check the time that's displayed on the dashboard. If we spend a grand total of *zero* minutes at home, we'll return to the Hollow Oak Beach House at 5:24. That gives us *plenty* of time before the bridal party starts getting ready at nine… but possibly not enough time before someone wakes up and notices the missing car. Keeping that in mind, speed is key.

"Can this thing go any faster?" I ask McCall.

"I'm going 50, and I don't know how much faster this old thing can really go. I was all for this crazy idea in my sleep-deprived state, but now I'm beginning to rethink things."

I glance out my window, watching as we pass the *'Welcome to Whitefield!'* sign. "Well, it's a little too late to turn around now."

I get a weird feeling as we pull up to my house. The last time I drove through my neighborhood, I was silently stressed. I had just run into Jesse at Wonderland Books and fibbed to him about having a plus one when that certainly was *not* the case. I then saw Cole in his driveway… and the rest is history.

Yet now, as McCall puts the gearshift into park, there's not another soul in sight. She opts to wait for me in the car, and I practically jump out of the passenger seat. I scramble for my house key, trying to fit it into the lock. Attempting to save as much time as possible, I rush upstairs and take the steps two at a time. When I reach my closet, I swing open the doors and slide all my clothes and empty hangers to the side. Hanging all the way to the right is the white garment bag that holds the reason for this secret rescue mission. I obtain it and hug it close.

The bottom of my bedroom blinds are raised, and I can see the light shining from Cole's window from here. The want and need to talk to him still weighs heavy on my chest, but I'm not sure how to do so without banging on his front door and waking up the entire Baxter family before 4 AM. With no time to waste, I force myself out of my room and down the stairs.

His stuff was still in Sunrise Beach, I remind myself. He surely has plans to go back, right?

I hurry through the living room and swing open the front door. Along with its familiar creak, I'm met with a familiar face. Dumbfoundedly, I think my mouth drops when I see him.

Cole.

Chapter 43

IN THE REARVIEW

"Good morning," he expresses, leaning against the edge of the doorframe.

"Morning," I manage to get out. "What are you doing up so early? What are you doing *here*?"

"I *was* asleep," he pauses. "Well, kind of. I wasn't able to sleep much, but then I heard a vehicle outside. I looked out my window and saw *that*." He turns, pointing to the yellow Chevy Bel Air sitting in my driveway.

"Sorry about that," I chuckle.

"I leave you alone for six hours, and you steal a car?"

"It's a long story. McCall stole the car; I'm just the accomplice. I forgot my bridesmaid dress and—wait," I pause. "What are you doing *here*—back in Whitefield? Is everything okay? You disappeared in such a hurry last night after the fight, and I was thinking that…."

"Yeah, everything's okay now." Cole sighs. "My mom's car engine blew up last night and had to be towed."

"Oh my gosh!" I exclaim. "Is she okay?"

"Yeah, thankfully. My dad is in Arizona for work, and last night my siblings were scattered across town at soccer games and ballet. My mom was stranded without a vehicle and clearly upset, which resulted in my dad calling me in a panic."

I react slowly, piecing the story together. "So, *that's* why you left so quickly." Now, I feel slightly dramatic over how I reacted to his disappearing act.

"Yeah, sorry about that. But it's a good thing I left when I did because I barely made it in time to pick up Cassie."

My eyes travel to the forming bruise on his jaw. Where the skin was red last night, it's now a dark shade of purple. "Look," I begin. "About what happened last night…"

He must have noticed my fixation on his bruise because he lifts a hand to cover it up for just a moment. "It's nothing." He shrugs. "No need to worry about it."

I glance at him. "It's *something* to worry over, and I feel awful about it."

"No, I understand. I guess we just played our roles too well. Maybe it did just add more fuel to his fire when I didn't respond to him the other day."

"Oh!" I exclaim. "I almost forgot. Give me one second, I'll be back." I rush out to the car, place my dress in the backseat, and retrieve Cole's phone. McCall smirks at me from the driver's seat. I hurry back to him, extending his phone.

"How'd you get this? I've been looking everywhere for it."

"It was in the driveway back at the beach house. When I tried to call you, I found this instead."

"Thank you." He taps on the screen, and it lights up.

YOUR MESSAGE TO 'FIN   ' FAILED TO SEND.

"Ah," he lets out a brief sigh. "That makes more sense, now."

I look at him, confused.

"I thought you had ignored a text I sent. For over half an hour, I waited for you at the gazebo."

As our conversation lengthens, I can practically feel any spare time that McCall and I have now slipping away. Despite the long drive ahead of us, I can't will myself to take a step in the direction of the car. I listen intently as Cole continues.

"Then, I saw you with him. And if I'm being honest," he pauses, "seeing the two of you together again felt like a punch in the gut, especially since you were a no-show to me. I had some things that I wanted to tell you—*topics* that I wanted to..." he drifts off.

"What did you want to talk to me about?" I nervously ask, unsure if this news will be good or bad.

"*Well...*" he says shyly with the familiar smile that I've secretly grown to love.

As he pauses, I confess, "Before Jesse waltzed his way into our night, I was coming to look for you. I had some things I wanted to tell you too."

Cole grins. "You first."

"*Nuh-uh!*" I object with a smile. "You started first; I'll let you finish."

"Okay, that's fair. I feel slightly dramatic over last night."

I giggle. "*Same.*"

"But in my defense," he stops, lifting a finger. "I thought I got punched for a girl who didn't like me back."

I laugh nervously at his comment. Did Cole just open a door for a new conversation covering the possible *real* side of our relationship?

I see a flash of light, realizing McCall is trying to get my attention. Based on how long I've spent talking to Cole, we're way behind schedule. "Crap," I mutter.

Has Malik blown our cover? Does Uncle Malcolm know that we took his car? Has my mom realized that I'm missing in the middle of the night? Does Aunt Sheryl know that I've gone haywire on a miniature road trip to get my dress? There's a multitude of things that could go wrong if we don't get back soon, and I can't stick around here any longer for them to come to fruition.

"What's wrong?" Cole asks.

"We have to get back before anyone wakes up," I explain in a panic. "I hate to rush off like this, but we can't get caught—especially not today." I climb into the passenger seat.

"Oh, definitely," he exclaims. "Be careful on your drive, and watch out for anything sharp enough to pop a tire."

"Don't jinx us," McCall notes.

I chuckle. "Now that you have your phone back, I'll give you a call if we need a tow."

"Noted."

As McCall begins to back out of the driveway, I roll down the window and call out to Cole, "You and I still need to finish our conversation!"

"Tonight!" Cole responds with a wink.

We ride through my neighborhood like Bonnie and Clyde, yet I still have a wide grin on my face, the infamous dress in the backseat, and a little closure on the guy in the rearview.

Chapter 44

HAPPY WEDDING DAY!

The drive back feels so much longer with the time crunch and the fact that we're too scared to drive over the speed limit. We pull through the golden gates that precede the Hollow Oak Beach House at *5:41 AM*.

"Go, go, go," I urge McCall as we scurry out of the car before anyone can see us. I hope the roar of the engine wasn't loud enough to wake anyone, but we couldn't risk parking anywhere other than the original spot. The white garment bag waves behind me as I run toward the house.

"*Shoot,*" McCall whispers, stopping in her tracks.

My words are cut short when I notice what's caused her to falter—or rather, *who*. Aunt Sheryl is the last person we wanted to get caught by this morning, and yet here she is. With a coffee mug in hand, she's sitting on the front porch swing, almost as though she's waiting for us to return. When I spot her eyes looking back at mine, I nearly gasp. *Of course*, we are too late. "Aunt Sheryl," I begin and try to hide the bag behind my back. "It's a long story, but I promise we can explain."

She lifts her free hand, cutting me off. "No need to explain, girls. Today's a very big day, and I'm going to pretend like I didn't see *whatever it is* that the two of you were up to."

"So, you're not going to mention this to anyone?" McCall cautions.

"Like who, your parents?" Aunt Sheryl nearly chuckles. "Both of your mothers and I did much worse when we were younger. Consider this our little secret." She points at me and presumably, points at the bag I did an awful job of hiding. "Besides, it looks like you had a good enough reason."

I want to run and tackle her in a grateful hug. Instead, I let out a relieved, "*Thank you.*"

McCall hurries to put away the car keys, and I practically sprint upstairs to our bedroom. Luckily enough, everyone else in the house seems to still be asleep.

As she walks into our room and closes the door, McCall states, "Malik is an awful lookout. Without any warning, we waltzed straight up to Aunt Sheryl. I'll have to give him an earful, for sure."

I plop onto the bed, and my bunny slippers drop to the floor. "Count me out. I'm taking a nap first."

"I second that."

With just a little over three hours until we meet up with the girls for hair and makeup, McCall and I are finally able to get the rest we undoubtedly need. As Aunt Sheryl said, *today is a very big day.*

I'm on my way to meet the rest of the bridal party when I hear Aunt Sheryl's voice echoing from downstairs. I glimpse over the balcony and spot her in the dining room, talking to a man whom I've never seen before. He's wearing a forest green shirt and holding a giant bouquet of lavender flowers.

"I'm not paying for the extras," Aunt Sheryl interjects. "However, I will gladly take them on behalf of your mistake."

"Look," he begins with one arm raised in surrender, "I'm just the temporary delivery man. My wife is the boss, but she's on maternity leave—just had a baby last week. All I was asked to do was deliver them and collect the final payment."

"Okay, but just because someone made a mistake and made twice as many floral arrangements as we ordered, doesn't mean that I'm *paying* double. That's on you." Perhaps it's the caffeine talking, but she seems to be back to her usual, somewhat snippy self.

Slowly, the guy nods. "I understand. Since we weren't able to make the delivery yesterday, maybe we can come to an agreement. Besides, my wife will kill me if I go back with a truckload of leftovers, and I really don't want to be the next spotlight on a murder mystery. I can see the headline now... *Death by a Thousand Rose Thorn Cuts.*"

Aunt Sheryl begins to smile. "I would love to take them off your hands... for the price we previously agreed on?"

The guy's wife surely won't be happy with that option, but he seems to begrudgingly agree. As one marriage is starting today, another may be on the brinks after this ordeal. I turn on my heels and quit eavesdropping on their conversation.

When I walk into the common area, I take notice of how it's transformed into what looks like a bridal suite. The walls are now lined with mirrors, and a gold clothing rack sits off to the side, holding the bridesmaids' dresses.

Sierra's wedding dress hangs separately. Even though I was there when she said *yes to the dress*, I still can't get over how fitting it is for her. It's a square-neck, silk dress with thin straps and a long train that flows onto the floor.

My eyes scan the room, taking in everything and everyone. McCall, Caroline, and Blaire all match in lavender robes. Sierra is slowly pacing the room in a satin, white robe.

With my arms spread out to her, I exclaim, "Happy Wedding Day!"

She squeals, wrapping me in an enthusiastic hug. "Thanks, Fin! I'm glad you're a part of it."

"Me too! Have you heard any news on Peyton?"

"Yes! She had the baby around two this morning. Let me show you the picture!"

She scurries for her phone and taps on the text icon. This image brings me back to my chat with Cole, the text I didn't get, and the conversation we started early this morning but never got to finish. *Tonight*, I remind myself. *He'll be here tonight.*

Sierra turns her phone around, showing me the screen. "Aww," I coo. He is perfect with a headful of dark hair and chubby cheeks that make you want to kiss him all over. "He is *adorable!*"

McCall scoots in to take a peek as well. "Isn't he just the cutest thing?"

"I know, right? I can't wait to meet him." Sierra responds.

"How's Juniper?" I question.

"She's doing good! Grandma Rose has gone full mother hen," she chuckles. "Peyton and Matt's families are driving in from D.C., so they'll be here later to pick up Juniper."

Wren walks into the room with her arms raised in the air. "Let's get ready for a wedding, people!" The rest of us chuckle, and we begin to do just that.

I've curled my hair to the best of my ability, which shockingly looks better than ever before. Maybe it's the water here, or maybe it's just the fancy hair products I've borrowed. Once it's sprayed with more than enough hairspray, Caroline begins to work her magic on my makeup. I can only hope that her art skills will cover the bags that have formed under my eyes.

"This anticipation is killing me," Sierra says.

I chuckle. "I could only imagine. I'm not the one getting married, and the anticipation is killing *me*."

Chapter 45

GORGEOUS

The pre-wedding hustle and bustle is in full swing. Due to last night's rain shower, people are now scattered about, setting up the venue.

Large canopies are being set up on the beach, adorned with chandeliers and fairy lights. A separate crew is piecing together a large dance floor beside the back patio. Chairs are being placed in the sand, mapping out the future aisle. Serving as the focal point for the ceremony, stems and petals are covering every inch of the altar. This only makes everything feel more real.

With the mix of lavender petals, light greenery, and pops of white, flowers are *everywhere*. The florists buzz around, filling every empty space. Our bouquets have been delivered to the upstairs bridal suite, and the flower petals perfectly match our dresses. The centerpieces for each table look like a miniature garden. And yet, there are still *many* flowers left over. Aunt

Sheryl makes the executive decision to add the extras onto the cute, little gazebo that's close enough to the reception area.

With her loose updo, natural but breathtaking makeup, stunning gown, and most importantly, her beaming expression, Sierra looks absolutely gorgeous.

The room is crammed with all the women in the house as Sierra adds the finishing touches. Once they add her dainty jewelry and tie the bow on the back of her dress, there isn't a single dry eye in the room… and that includes Peyton, who is on a video chat from her labor and delivery room.

"*Sierra*," Aunt Sheryl begins through watery eyes. "You look beautiful, baby."

"Mom…." Sierra's voice waivers. "Don't make me cry. We just finished my makeup!"

I stand at the top of the staircase, arm in arm with a guy whom I just met moments ago. I don't even remember his name… Lawson, Landon, Logan? *Logan*

—that's it! As McCall reaches the bottom step and begins to walk down the aisle, Logan and I step in unison, one stair at a time.

I try to focus as the sea of faces is looking back, all eyes on us. I see one in particular that stands out among the rest. *He made it here!* In his dark grey suit, Cole watches me with a smile, and I feel the one on my face grow in size. *So much for focusing.*

Chapter 46

NOT-SO-SECRET

The ceremony is absolutely stunning—an ethereal scene of calm waves, a baby blue sky, and an altar engulfed in flowers. As Sierra and Dalton get hitched, everything goes off without a hitch.

The new Mr. and Mrs. Bray make their grand entrance into the reception area. As people join them on the dance floor, I set out to find Cole. However, I'm stopped by chatty family members before I can find him.

The questions are endless. My second cousin, Charissa, is dying to know where I found my quote-unquote *dazzling* high heels. They were a steal, only $10 from a local boutique. Yet, they're already killing my feet, so I wouldn't recommend them.

Grandma Rose's brother wants to know how I enjoyed my college semester in New York. I inform him that I just graduated high school and have never been to New York, although it is on my bucket list. He suggests a long list of places to visit on my future trip, such as the *Strand Book Store* and the *Statue of Liberty*.

An older lady makes a comment about how tall I've gotten as I walk past her table. I politely agree, although I don't recall ever meeting her. She then stands and asks for directions to the restroom, which I promptly give, pointing her in the right direction.

As I turn to continue my search and try not to make eye contact with anyone else, I nearly bump into him. My eyes meet Cole's, and he's standing directly in front of me.

"*Oh*," I say, slightly surprised. "Hi."

"Hey," he replies. "You look beautiful."

"Thank you! I'm glad you made it," I cheerily say.

Cole lets out a low laugh. "Yeah… I made it by the skin of my teeth. Who knew that a soccer tournament for six-year-olds could last *so long*? Luckily Chase's team won, so it wasn't all for nothing."

"Aww, that's great!" My eyes travel to the purple bruise on his jaw. Unless I'm imagining it, it's even darker now than it was early this morning. I gesture a hand with a small grimace. "Would you let me attempt to cover that up? I feel guilty every time I look at it."

He furrows his brows. "Why do you feel guilty?"

I shrug. "Jesse was my mess. So if you really think about it, it's my fault."

"Nonsense," Cole smiles. "I think I warranted the punch all on my own when I called him a liar and told him he treated you like crap."

"Fifty-fifty," I joke.

It takes some convincing for him to believe that the makeup won't have him looking like a clown. Once he agrees, we head upstairs, and I grab my makeup bag.

We sit in silence as I add dabs of concealer onto his jaw. As I lean close to him, I notice all of his features —the sculpted edges of his jaw, the lone freckle on his cheekbone that's so small I've never noticed it before, and his eyelashes that are even longer than mine.

I apply one more drop of concealer, blend it in, and try to make it look as seamless with the rest of his skin as possible. My skin tone is naturally lighter, so I blend in a darker shade to help match his. "There you go," I say. "I think that's about as good as it's going to get."

He glances in the mirror, nodding satisfactorily. "Not bad, Fin. I no longer look like I got sucker punched."

I shoot him a glare. "Don't remind me."

We join the party, mixing ourselves in with the fun chaos. After *horribly* dancing with Cole to your typical wedding songs, the DJ announces that it's time for the bouquet toss.

"Come on!" McCall exclaims, pulling me away from Cole and toward the forming crowd. I jolt forward, following her lead without much choice.

Sierra stands at the head of the crowd, bouquet in hand. The DJ calls out, "1… 2… 3!", and the bouquet flies into the air.

I take a large step before feeling a snap and ungracefully falling to the floor. Apparently, my bargain heels don't hold up all too well. I'm on the floor, surrounded by girls who are fumbling with the bouquet... when it lands with a heap in my lap.

Loud claps and cheers erupt. All I can do is throw my head back in laughter, with a bouquet in one hand and a broken heel in the other.

I try to hide my embarrassment as I stand with the crowd's attention still partially on me. Hopefully, the layers of makeup on my face cover the natural blush that has formed.

"Finley!" Sierra runs up to me, giggling. "You poor thing."

McCall jokes, "Hey, at least you caught the bouquet!"

"It only cost me a shoe and my pride," I chuckle. "I think you jinxed me with how much you talked about falling."

We walk over to the table with our names on the placeholders and grab a much-needed glass of water. We take a seat just in time for the garter toss. As the sea of unmarried men takes center stage, I don't see Cole standing in the mix.

Taking a sip of my drink, I turn to McCall. "Have you seen Cole?"

"I thought you'd never ask," she says with a smirk.

"What do you mean?"

She outstretches a folded piece of paper in her hand. "I was told to give you this. It seems you have a *not-so-secret* admirer."

I grin as I unfold the paper and read the contents inside.

F—

I believe we have a conversation to finish.

Gazebo @ 7:30...
FOR REAL THIS TIME ??

—C

Chapter 47

FOR REAL THIS TIME

I glance up at McCall. "Maybe you *can* keep a secret."

Lightly, she nudges my arm. "I'm just full of surprises. Now *go*! Go get your boyfriend." She winks as she pushes me toward the sand.

With the last rays of the sunset and the now distant reception serving as my only sources of light, my bare feet run in the sand. Off in the distance, I see Cole waiting at the gazebo.

It's not until I reach it that I realize just how many flowers have been placed here. Each pillar is overflowing with a mixture of purple and ivory roses. With his back to me, Cole is standing at the heart of the floral haven.

I tiptoe up the steps and gently tap him on the shoulder.

He spins, turning to face me.

"I heard that we have a conversation to finish?"

Cole smiles. "You heard correctly."

"So," I start, suddenly nervous. "Where do we begin?"

He looks nearly as jittery as I feel, although he's trying to compose himself—*as am I*. After taking a deep breath, he begins by saying, "Last night when I tried to meet you here, I had a lot that I wanted to talk about. Rather, I had a lot that I wanted to say about *us*."

My hands fidget with my two-day-old manicure, unsure of what else to do while he's talking.

"With the whole fake dating thing... I can't do it anymore, Fin."

My heart begins to sink. After saying all the things he did this morning and showing up here this evening, I was *so sure* that our feelings were the same. Now, I'm beginning to question everything once again. "Wait, what are you saying?" I ask.

"I can't fake date you because it's not *fake* to me anymore."

I can only manage an, "*Oh*," as the familiar, small glimmer of hope finds its way back to me.

"I don't know how you feel, but for me... I can't pretend any longer. I can't keep holding your hand and almost kissing you."

"Twice," I point out with a minuscule smile.

"Right," Cole grins shyly. "I can't almost kiss you *twice* just to walk away from it all in a few days."

"Cole...."

"I'm sorry, but I can't. A week ago, you said that we could '*fake it till we make it through the week*'. But honestly? I feel like we've made it... and it feels too real to me. I wish that we could—"

Before he has the chance to say anything further, I blurt out, "It's not fake for me, either."

His gaze softens.

"No offense, but up until this week, I'd only ever thought of you as a friend. I truthfully planned for it to stay that way, but then...." I pause. "The next thing I knew, I was holding your hand and being dragged into the ocean and—"

"For the last time, I definitely carried you!" he interjects.

I correct myself. "But then I was being *carried* into the ocean. We slow danced in the diner like a couple of dorks, you planned the best date I've ever been on, and out of nowhere... everything started to feel real."

He takes my hands in his, and it automatically calms my fidgety nerves.

"I can't do it, either," I say, shaking my head. "Not if it's fake—not if *we* are."

Cole takes a small step closer to me. "Then maybe we can be... for real this time."

I take a step of my own and keep my eyes fixated on his. "For real this time? I think I'd like that."

Cole lets go of one hand to tuck a strand of hair behind my ear just as he had done days ago. The movement sends a chill of *not-so-mythical* butterflies through my body. With each nanosecond that passes, the fluttery feeling increases.

We lean forward until our foreheads touch.

"Wait," he expresses with a smile on his lips.

I pull back slightly, looking up at him. "Hmm?"

"Are you sure you don't need to practice first?" he jokes, showing the same mischievous smirk I've grown fond of. "I mean, you *did* have to practice holding my hand so that you didn't laugh."

I roll my eyes with a chuckle. "Oh, shut up and just kiss me already!"

As the small space between us closes, I know that the small space between the words *boy* and *friend* close too. This time, we're no longer pretending. In fact, I think it's the most real feeling that I've ever felt.

Maybe it's true—*the third time's a charm.*

Chapter 48

PLOT TWIST

With his hand on the side of my face and my unspoken words finally out in the open, I feel as though everything's going to be okay. This time, I truly believe it. The thought of a broken relationship doesn't come to mind.

Although perhaps… some things need to be broken in order to be mended.

Even though I thought that I had not been brokenhearted—maybe I needed to get my heart broken to feel whole again. Perhaps I needed to go through the pain to see the good that waited on the other side—or rather, to see *who* was waiting—the guy who grew up on the other side of the fence in my backyard, the other side of the minivan on our rides to school, and the other side of the door when I needed someone to talk to.

Maybe I was supposed to have an ex-boyfriend with a shattered ego to show me what I *didn't* want.

Maybe I needed to find someone new to show me what I *do* want—someone to show me the way I deserve to be treated, even when it means breaking our own rules.

Maybe I needed to break my cheap pair of heels so that I could run even faster out to Cole.

The twinkling stars fill the midnight blue sky. As the night continues to grow darker, the gazebo lights up with countless strands of fairy lights. They twist up and down each pillar, illuminating our own little world.

I share a look with Cole, both of us grinning from ear to ear. After everything that's happened between us, my heart is practically beating out of my chest in the best way possible.

Just as I'm thinking to myself that this moment can't get any better... it does. Contrasting against the dark sky, a golden light floats overhead. Then another. And another. Within a matter of seconds, dozens upon dozens of paper lanterns float into the air. They fill the night sky, making a constellation of their own. Sierra had described her plan for the lantern release, but I never expected the fairytale image to feel so real.

Cole lifts my chin, and I quickly kiss him once more. Everything—the two of *us*, in particular—still feels like a vivid dream. It's one that I'll surely wake up from in a matter of minutes, wondering what would have happened if it were true. Excitedly, I smile—because it's not a dream. I'll stay awake, living fully in this moment, and I'll figure out where this leads us. *We* will figure it out together.

"Out of everyone you could've asked to be your fake boyfriend, I'm glad you chose me," he admits.

As I rest my head just below his chin, I respond, "There's no one else I would rather be here with. I'm glad you saved this little ole' damsel in distress, after all."

"What can I say? I'm all about you, Princess."

I shake my head with a smile, but I don't even mention his use of the horrid nickname. I have a feeling I'm going to have to get used to them eventually.

With the distant sounds of music playing at the reception, we slowly rock together. As I look out past the horizon, I think that maybe I've reached it—*the plot twist*—the turning point in my story. It has uprooted my plans for what is to come… and my plot twist is the guy holding onto me.

I have no clue what's in store for me on the next page, and still… *I turn it anyway.*

SUNDAY
The Day After the Wedding

SUNDAY *playlist*

- Coastline ———————————— Hollow Coves
- Need The Sun To Break ————— James Bay
- Whatever Forever ——————— The Mowgli's
- Ily ———————————————— HARBOUR
- The blue ————————————— Gracie Abrams
- Ho Hey ———————————— The Lumineers
- We Are Family ————————— Sister Sledge
- Finally Free ————————— Joshua Bassett
- Moments We Live For ————— In Paradise
- Run (Taylor's Version) (From The Vault) ———
  ———————————— Taylor Swift, Ed Sheeran
- We're Going Home ——————— Vance Joy
- Shotgun ————————————— George Ezra
- More Than Friends ————— Aidan Bissett

Chapter 49

SUNRISE BEACH

Last night, amidst the chaos of wedding activities and shared kisses, I had the realization that in all our days spent in Sunrise Beach, we've yet to actually *watch* the sunrise. We've witnessed the sunsets, blue skies, and dark nights, but we haven't watched as the day comes to life.

Cole and I watch from the Adirondack chairs near the water. Both of us are bundled up in blankets, attempting to combat the frosty morning air.

I do my best to suffice a yawn, yet I fail. The wedding festivities had everyone still awake in the early morning hours. Ignoring my body's craving for more than three hours of sleep, I forced myself out of bed. After all, this is our last chance to watch the sunrise here.

The sun begins to break the water's surface. As the bright orange glow ascends from beneath the horizon, the colors grow more and more vibrant.

Cole turns his attention away from the view and onto me. Outstretching his hand, he says, "I want to spend the rest of my sunrises with you."

As I take his hand in mine, I can't contain my quiet laughter. "That sounds magical," I manage through giggles. "You're pretty cheesy, but your attempt at romanticism is great."

I look back at the horizon, watching as new colors bloom. I think I've found it—the place that feels golden and bright. The place I've been searching for.

"It's so pretty!" A voice echoes. McCall and Malik sprint out the back door.

My hand leaves Cole's, both of us silently agreeing that the romantic start to our day is now over. Even so, I'm happy to have my cousins temporarily interrupt us.

As they make their way out to us, I pat my lap and gesture for McCall to sit down. I scoot over, sharing my blanket with her as we both cram onto the small seat.

Malik turns to Cole with pleading eyes. "*Nuh-uh*," Cole objects, shaking his head. "No way you're sitting on my lap. Go get your own chair."

Instead, Malik just plops down onto the damp sand. McCall gives him a questionable look. With a shrug, Malik says, "Would you rather me sit on your lap?"

"*No!*" McCall and I loudly say in unison.

I take in the view that's in front of me and the people who are around me, and I don't ever want to forget this moment.

Unlike footprints in the sand... it's an impression that's here to stay.

an impression thats here to stay

Chapter 50

THE END OF AN ERA

For one last time, everyone joins together outside the Hollow Oak Beach House. Cars are being filled with suitcases as we prepare to leave this incredible week behind.

Cole shuts the back door after putting in the last of our luggage. I slowly walk up to Sierra with open arms, not wanting this week to end. She envelops me in a tight hug as soon as I reach her. "Thank you for having us here," I say, genuinely grateful for our time spent together.

"Aww, of course," she coos. "I had a blast with all of you."

"Me too! It felt like our old sleepovers, only way more glamorous."

McCall jogs up to us. "Group hug!"

We chuckle, the three of us coming together like old times. Dalton stands behind Sierra, so we shuffle over to add him into the mix. Happily, he joins us—now a part of our crazy family.

Afterward, McCall and I chat for a moment, like we haven't had enough of one another this week. We will both be moving away to college in the fall, but luckily, our campuses are only thirty minutes apart. Our future schools may be rivals, but neither of us could be more excited to finally live so close. We shared many nights this week searching for apartments online, so we can continue having childish sleepovers into our adult lives.

Malik and Cole join us, and I have the sad realization that the four of us won't be together for quite some time. On the first day of this trip, it was odd to see Cole join our group. Now, he's practically completed the 'core four'. The thought makes me smile.

As we're saying our bittersweet goodbyes and wrapping up our conversation, Uncle Malcolm walks up to us. "I know what you did this summer," he states.

We all share a worried glance, seemingly knowing what he's talking about—*his prized possession*.

"I know about the Bel Air, but would any of you like to fess up?"

Another glance gets passed our circle, yet no one says a word.

Malik is the first to move, yet he only lunges for Cole. "Tag, you're it!" he calls, sprinting off.

"Hey!" Cole yells. "Unfair advantage!"

"You owed me a rematch!" Malik calls from all the way out in the sand.

Slyly, Cole turns to me. "Weren't we up for a rematch too?"

I smile. "Don't do it."

He reaches for me, and I yelp. Taking McCall's hand, I pull her with me as we sprint toward Malik and away from the truth. We're running around like a bunch of children, and I watch as Uncle Malcolm shakes his head from the driveway. So much for any of us confessing… *today.*

Now exhausted, I pause for a moment to catch my breath. Glancing up, I take a final look at the grand, white Hollow Oak Beach House. In a weird way, I feel like I need to tell the house goodbye as well. Through everything, it has been a part of this week nearly as much as everyone else.

Looking at it now, it's like a giant kaleidoscope of memories.

The rooftop—where Cole brought me to say that he was clueless about how to answer my grandmother's questions surrounding our relationship.

The bedroom—where McCall and I shared a great amount of laughter but also where she comforted me as I shed a few tears.

The kitchen—where Cole and I managed to start an oven fire, and McCall and Malik burnt French toast to a crisp.

The upstairs common area—where we watched Sierra get ready for her big day, and not a single soul had dry eyes.

The living area—where we ran inside after our possum encounter and where flowers were constantly being delivered through the grand doors.

And lastly, but certainly not least... *the gazebo.* The gazebo—where we all raced to, where Cole and I escaped with the final slices of pizza, and where everything fake became real under a haze of fairy lights, paper lanterns, and an array of florals. The gazebo—where yet another rule was broken for the better.

After sorrowfully saying our final goodbyes, Cole and I are on our way back home.

With one hand on the steering wheel, Cole is taking a sip of his soda when he hits a bump in the street. This sends the brown, sticky liquid splashing all over him. He mutters something under his breath before asking, "Can you see if we have any napkins in the glove box?" Luckily, he's wearing a black shirt, so the developing stain isn't noticeable.

I dig through the compartment and grab a wrinkled napkin from the heap of papers. "Here you go."

Just as I'm shutting the door, something catches my eye. I pull it out, immediately giggling.

"What's up?" he asks, briefly turning to me before fixating his eyes back on the road.

I straighten some of the crumbled edges of the receipt. "*Rule #1,*" I begin.

"Oh no," Cole chuckles.

I laugh. "We didn't follow our rules too well."

Cole nonchalantly waves his hand in the air. "Eh, I've always been *quite* the rule breaker."

MONDAY

3 Weeks Later...

MONDAY *playlist*

- Home ———————————— Phillip Phillips
- Teenage Dream ————————— Stephen Dawes
- Paradise ———————————————— Bazzi
- Everything We Need ——— A Day To Remember
- Loverboy —————————————— A-Wall
- This One ————————————— Vance Joy
- Daydream ——————————— Milk & Bone
- The Love Club ———————————— Lorde
- Sold out of Love ——————— The Nude Party
- Wonderland ———————————— Taylor Swift
- All Day ——————————————— Jack Botts

Chapter 51

THE RABBIT HOLE

A knock sounds from the other side of my bedroom door. "Come in!" I call out. There's no answer from the hall, so I try again. "You can come in!" A few seconds pass with no response, so I place my bookmark between the pages of my current read and get up to open the door.

Saylor is hiding in the hallway, snickering. I smile at the sight of the folded piece of paper she's holding out to me. I know *exactly* who this is from.

"Delivery!" she chimes.

I grab the paper with a quick thanks. She skips back down the hallway as soon as it's out of her grasp. Unfolding it, I read…

F—

-RULE #1: Don't be late for a very important date!

-RULE #2: Meet me @11:30 where you fell down the rabbit hole.

— C

Refolding the note, I place it in my dresser drawer and add it to the collection that's grown over the last few weeks.

Within a few minutes, I'm out the door and driving to the only place I can think of that fits the '*down the rabbit hole*' clue.

I arrive earlier than planned, and I don't see any signs of Cole in the parking lot. Since I have time to spare, I decide to browse the shelves of Wonderland Books. I could happily spend all day within the walls of a bookstore, getting sucked into lives and worlds different from my own.

Although I have a stack of unread books at home and should probably be on a book-buying ban, I head straight to the romance section. I crouch down, searching the bottom shelf for something that may spark my interest.

I grab a paperback and quickly stand up to read the synopsis when my rear end bumps directly into someone. "Oh!" I exclaim, shocked. "I'm so sorry!" Spinning on my heels, I spot a familiar face with long, dark brown hair. "Hey, Skye," I say with a polite smile.

Skye Williams is a year older than me, so until I ran into her at the Starwoods Summer Camp, I hadn't seen her much since she graduated last spring. Saylor attends camp a few days a week, and Skye is typically the one to sign her out during pick-up. On occasion, we've gotten to chat briefly.

"Finley, hi!" She smiles. "I'm sorry about that. I wasn't watching where I was going."

I wave a hand, brushing it off. "Oh, no worries. It was all my butt's fault."

Skye chuckles.

"There you are!" Another familiar face exasperates, turning to Skye. I recognize her immediately as Becca Holland. While Skye was always a little more reserved in high school, Becca has always been the free spirit. "I've been looking *everywhere* for you. I couldn't see you over the labyrinth of shelves."

Skye gives her a questionable look. "I just walked away from you literally two seconds ago."

Becca shrugs. "Grayson just texted me. He and Brody are waiting whenever we're ready."

"Sounds good," Skye responds before turning to me. "Would you want to come with us? We're going to get pizza at Josephine's."

"Aw, I totally would, but I'm actually waiting for someone. Thanks for asking, though!"

"Yeah, of course! Another day?"

I smile. "Sounds great!"

We exchange a quick goodbye, and then they're both on their way. The door chimes as they walk out, and perhaps the most familiar face walks in.

I walk over to him and place my hand in his as we stand next to the display table of local authors. "So, what's on our agenda for the rest of the day?"

Cole grins. "Where's the fun if you know what we're going to be doing? Broken rules and unexpected plans seem to be our thing."

EPILOGUE

5 Years Later...

EPILOGUE *playlist*

- forever & more ———————— ROLE MODEL
- Heaven ———————— Niall Horan
- the 1 ———————————— Taylor Swift
- Rollercoaster ————————————— Bleachers
- Love Story (Taylor's Version) ———— Taylor Swift
- We Are Young ————————— fun., Janelle Monáe
- Coastline ————————————— Hollow Coves
- Long Live ———————————— Taylor Swift
- The One ———————————————— Kodaline
- Let's Get Married ————————— Bleachers
- Daylight ——————————————— Taylor Swift
- I'm with You ——————————————— Vance Joy
- be my forever ——— Christina Perri, Ed Sheeran
- My Everyday ————————————— Volunteer
- Ours ——————————————— Taylor Swift
- Where It All Begins ———— Summer Kennedy
- long story short ———————— Taylor Swift

Epilogue

LONG STORY SHORT

We knew. I knew after the week we spent at the beach house with fake dates and floating lanterns. Cole says he knew long before that, but I'm still not sure how much I believe him. Either way, we both knew it was coming *eventually...* we just wanted to wait for the right time.

So, after four years away at college, study dates in the library, and then another year of getting ourselves settled into a somewhat normal life—*we're back*. We've come into town quite a few times, and we have even pulled the occasional all-nighter to drive here from campus—specifically for the sunrise.

After all, they're a different kind of magic in Sunrise Beach.

"Hey there, Fin," I hear Cole's voice from behind me.

I cover my eyes with a squeal. "You can't look at me!"

"I'm not!" he replies. "Trust me when I say that *I want to*, but your Maid of Honor is serving as a human shield, making sure I don't steal so much as a peek. Not to mention, there's a house—sorry, *two* houses—full of relatives who would personally remind me of every superstitious curse."

Even with my hand still covering my eyes, I can perfectly visualize McCall's smile through her words. "You're good to look at the sunrise now. Just don't turn around."

I open my eyes toward the horizon. I'm now two for two when it comes to waking up way too early on wedding days....

Only this wedding happens to be mine.

"Do you have any pre-wedding thoughts, Cole?" I ask.

"I have super glue in the pocket of my tux—just in case your heel breaks again."

"Aww, you're always my knight in shining armor who comes to my rescue. I'm glad I fell *head over broken heels* for you all those years ago."

"That makes two of us." He chuckles quietly. "Don't be late for our most important date."

"Oh, don't you worry—I'll be *ready*."

I'll be ready... to sprint into a blossoming life with Cole by my side, to sign the lease on our new house in Sunrise Beach, to run into the ocean and ignore screams of ruining my wedding dress. I'll be ready to sign the paperwork for a little white building in town and name it *Baxter & Brook's Books* now that I've found my business partner—*my life partner.*

Cole was my first boy friend. Boy. *Space.* Friend. Jesse was my first boyfriend. No spaces—and no regrets since he led me here. Cole, on the other hand, was my first plot twist and my first fake boyfriend. Most importantly, Cole is my first—*and my only*—forever.

With my eyes on the glimmering horizon, my mind races with thoughts of new beginnings as Cole and I create even more stories together. The new chapter in our lives begins tonight. It may be just another happily ever after, but this one is *ours.*

Long story short, we're just getting started.

The End
—— OR ——
The Beginning

Long story short,
were just getting started.

ACKNOWLEDGMENTS

- When I think of acknowledgments, I like to think of them as the author's love letter. So, here's my handwritten love letter to all of you....

- To you, the person who's holding my book in your hands: Thank you! While writing this book, I wrote it for myself to continue to fulfill my lifelong dreams of being an author, but I also wrote it for you. I hope you found a piece of yourself within the pages of this book, & I hope you enjoyed!

- To my family: Mom, Dad, & Brooklyn: The three of you have shown me so much love & support in every aspect of my life, & for that I am forever grateful. You've supported me in all of my writing endeavors, even when it was short stories I was writing at 10 years old. I'm so glad that you're the first people I get to share all of my wild ideas with, along with the first people who get to see them come to fruition. There's so much more I could say, but I'll end by saying that I love you all beyond the 56,000 words in this book!

- Thanks to the "strangers on the internet" who certainly do not feel like strangers any longer: Morgan, Kristyn, Makenna, Zoe, Kayla, Charissa, Julia, Ris, Emma, Jennah, Tiffany, Jennifer, Katie,

Emily, Maddie, Corina, & so many incredible others. Seeing all of your comments & messages have meant so much to me!⌣

- To all of the people who make videos about my books, leave kind reviews, & share my indie books with others: I'm contiously blown away by the love & support that I'm shown from you all!

- To all of you who dream of writing a book of your own: JUST DO IT!!! It's so heartwarming when I have someone message me for writing/aspiring author advice. I'm certainly no expert, but the biggest advice I have is to just do it! Believe me, two years ago I had zero clue what I was doing... & I've lived by the quote "fake it till you make it" ever since. ⌣ Brainstorm ideas, run the notes app on your phone dry, let the words find you, & fake it... with hopes that one day you'll make it.

- There are so many others who I could thank who felt like they were alongside me when writing this book. Taylor Swift, who I've grown up with from country back roads to writing at midnight. I'll forever love your invisible string of perfect lyricism. I want to thank authors such as Lynn Painter & Morgan Matson, whose stories & way with words have inspired me endlessly. Along with other artists, such as Vance Joy, Olivia Rodrigo, Jenny Han, KL Walther, Joshua Bassett, Gracie Abrams, & many others who have served as inspirations.

• Lastly, I want to thank Head Over Broken Heels as a whole. This book was made with so much endless love for these characters & this story. I had the most fun bringing Finley's story to life, whether that was drawing the cover & illustrations you'll find throughout this book, writing about a fake relationship, putting together a dozen playlists, brainstorming the best way to end a chapter, handwriting the chapter titles, or a multitude of other things. To Finley, Cole, McCall, Malik, & the rest of the Sunrise Beach Crew—I love you all! I can't wait to see what's in store for everyone next.

• Once again, thank YOU for helping to make my dreams a reality. Getting to write books like this has felt like my own ~~happily~~ ever after.

♡Haley

ALL SONGS

- long story short ——————— Taylor Swift
- People Watching ——————— Conan Gray
- Unwritten ————— Natasha Bedingfield
- We Are Never Ever Getting Back Together
  (Taylor's Version) ——————— Taylor Swift
- Bad Love ———————————— Dehd
- Anything Could Happen ———— Ellie Goulding
- Mary's Song (Oh My My My) ——— Taylor Swift
- Don't Fade ——————————— Vance Joy
- Backyard Boy ————— Claire Rosinkranz
- The Story of Us ——————— Taylor Swift
- Someone New ————————— Hozier
- This Could Be Good ————— Morningsiders
- Something That I Want ———— Grace Potter
- Come With Me ———— Surfaces, Salem ilese
- Boyfriend ————————————— COIN
- Karma ——————————— Taylor Swift
- Saturday Sun ——————— Vance Joy
- Come To The Beach — Winnetka Bowling League
- Vacation ———————— The Go-Go's

- Almost (Sweet Music) ———————— Hozier
- Sit Next to Me ——————— Foster The People
- Dirty Little Secret ——— The All-American Rejects
- Dover Beach ———————— Baby Queen
- Mastermind ———————— Taylor Swift
- Cool Kids ———————— Echosmith
- Destination ——————— Nickel Creek
- Fun ———————————— Sun Room
- Heartbreak Yellow ——————— Andy Davis
- Supermassive Black Hole —————— Muse
- Just Friends ———————— Jonas Brothers
- Call It What You Want ————— Taylor Swift
- Perfect Places ———————— Lorde
- Summerland —————————— half-alive
- Lover ———————————— Taylor Swift
- Ex's & Oh's ———————— Elle King
- Telling Myself ——————— Joshua Bassett
- Float ————————— HARBOUR
- I Ain't Worried ——————— OneRepublic
- Sunrise, Sunburn, Sunset ———— Luke Bryan
- I Want You ———————— Sun Room
- BRIGHTSIDE ————— The Lumineers
- Daydreaming ——————— Harry Styles
- Cruel Summer ——————— Taylor Swift
- The Tide ———————— Niall Horan
- stuck on us ——— Claire Rosinkranz, Aidan Bissett
- Feel Something ——————— Joshua Bassett
- Swim - Reprise ————————— Valley
- Dog Days Are Over ——— Florence + The Machine
- All Day All Night ——————— Moon Taxi

- My Girl ———————————— The Temptations
- 1 step forward, 3 steps back ——— Olivia Rodrigo
- Catalonia ———————————— Vance Joy
- Convertible in the Rain ———— Brynn Cartelli
- Play Pretend —————————— Alex Sampson
- Sh-Boom ———————————— The Chords
- Fearless (*Taylor's Version*) ————— Taylor Swift
- Bahamas ———————————— HARBOUR
- Coast ————— Hailee Steinfeld, Anderson .Paak
- Surfin' U.S.A. ————————— The Beach Boys
- Runaway Kids ————————— HARBOUR
- Sunshine —————————— OneRepublic
- Gimme! Gimme! Gimme! (A Man After Midnight) ———————————————————— ABBA
- Lavender Haze ————————— Taylor Swift
- Taylor Swift ————————— Matt Cooper
- Shut Up and Dance ——— WALK THE MOON
- invisible string ————————— Taylor Swift
- Really Wanna Dance With You ——— New Rules
- Head Over Heels ————— Tears For Fears
- Enchanted ——————————— Taylor Swift
- Don't Kill My Vibe ——————— Sigrid
- i'm too pretty for this ———— Claire Rosinkranz
- Gaslighter ———————————— The Chicks
- The Great War ————————— Taylor Swift
- Riptide ———————————— Vance Joy
- New Religion ————————— The Haydaze
- Mess It Up ————————— Gracie Abrams
- We Didn't Start the Fire ————— Billy Joel

- The Very First Night (*Taylor's Version*) (*From The Vault*) ──────────── Taylor Swift
- As It Was ──────────── Harry Styles
- The Idea of You ──────── Grady, lovelytheband
- THE LITTLE THINGS ──────── Kelsea Ballerini
- Dancing in the Moonlight ──────── Toploader
- Loverboy ──────────── A-Wall
- Snow On The Beach ── Taylor Swift, Lana Del Rey
- traitor ──────────── Olivia Rodrigo
- Happily ──────────── One Direction
- Looking At Me Like That ──────── Vance Joy
- Looking at Me ──────── Sabrina Carpenter
- She Will Be Loved ──────── Maroon 5
- WHERE WE ARE ──────── The Lumineers
- You Belong With Me (*Taylor's Version*) ────────
  ──────────── Taylor Swift
- Feels Like ──────── Gracie Abrams
- Nonsense ──────── Sabrina Carpenter
- That Feeling ──────── HARBOUR
- Flowers in Your Hair ──────── The Lumineers
- Love Like That ──────── Phillip Phillips
- Anyone Else ──────── Joshua Bassett
- Sweet Nothing ──────── Taylor Swift
- Boardwalk ──────── Vance Joy
- All Of The Girls You Loved Before ── Taylor Swift
- Young Lovers Do ──────── Tilly W
- If I Fall ──────────── Nick Jonas
- Heaven Falls/Fall On Me ──────── Surfaces
- My Type ──────── Saint Motel
- I'm Good ──────── The Mowgli's

- Love Song ——————————— Sara Bareilles
- Sweet Talk ——————————— Saint Motel
- Everything Has Changed (*Taylor's Version*) ———
  ——————————— Taylor Swift, Ed Sheeran
- Sweetheart (*Unreleased*) ——————— Joshua Bassett
- Satellite ——————————— Harry Styles
- this is what falling in love feels like ——— JVKE
- gold rush ——————————— Taylor Swift
- I Want You to Want Me ————— Cheap Trick
- Like Gold ——————————— Vance Joy
- Just for a Moment ———————————
  ——————— Olivia Rodrigo, Joshua Bassett
- We Made It ——————— Louis Tomlinson
- Glitch ——————————— Taylor Swift
- Different ——————————— Joshua Bassett
- Kiss Me While You Can (Unreleased) ———
  ——————————— Joshua Bassett
- I Think He Knows ——————— Taylor Swift
- I Think I'm In Love ——————— Kat Dahlia
- Speak Now ——————————— Taylor Swift
- Jessie's Girl ——————— Rick Springfield
- Little Lion Man ——————— Mumford & Sons
- Sue Me ——————— Sabrina Carpenter
- Watch Your Mouth ——— The Backseat Lovers
- Say You're Sorry ——————— Sara Bareilles
- Set Me Free ——————— Joshua Bassett
- I Did Something Bad ——————— Taylor Swift
- Bad Reputation ——— Joan Jett & the Blackhearts
- brutal ——————————— Olivia Rodrigo
- Vicious ——————— Sabrina Carpenter

- crashing down ———————————— Arlie
- Bruises ————————————— Lewis Capaldi
- All Too Well (*10 Minute Version*) (*Taylor's Version*)
  (*From The Vault*) ——————— Taylor Swift
- Solid Ground ————————————— Vance Joy
- The Good Ones ——————— Gabby Barrett
- Love Come Back To Me —————— Phillip Phillips
- Come Back… Be Here (*Taylor's Version*) ————
  ———————————————— Taylor Swift
- Ribs ——————————————— Lorde
- Hanging On The Telephone ——————— Blondie
- Take Me Home Tonight ————— Eddie Money
- Getaway Car ——————————— Taylor Swift
- Home To You ————————————Jack Botts
- All I Want ————————————— Kodaline
- For Your Love ————————— GUNNAR
- Beginning Middle End ——————— Leah Nobel
- Death By A Thousand Cuts ——————— Taylor Swift
- Lay It On Me ———————————— Vance Joy
- For Real This Time —————— Gracie Abrams
- Talk Too Much ——————————— COIN
- Kiss Her You Fool ———————— Kids That Fly
- Something That I Want —————— Grace Potter
- Never Felt A Love Like This—————————
  ———————— Galantis, Hook N Sling, Dotan
- long story short ——————————— Taylor Swift
- Missing Piece ————————————— Vance Joy
- Enchanted ——————————— Taylor Swift
- Someone To You-Acoustic ————— BANNERS
- I See the Light ———— Mandy Moore, Zachary Levi

- Today Was A Fairytale (Taylor's Version) ———— Taylor Swift
- Coastline ———— Hollow Coves
- Need The Sun To Break ———— James Bay
- Whatever Forever ———— The Mowgli's
- Ily ———— HARBOUR
- The blue ———— Gracie Abrams
- Ho Hey ———— The Lumineers
- We Are Family ———— Sister Sledge
- Finally Free ———— Joshua Bassett
- Moments We Live For ———— In Paradise
- Run (Taylor's Version) (From The Vault) ———— Taylor Swift, Ed Sheeran
- We're Going Home ———— Vance Joy
- Shotgun ———— George Ezra
- More Than Friends ———— Aidan Bissett
- Home ———— Phillip Phillips
- Teenage Dream ———— Stephen Dawes
- Paradise ———— Bazzi
- Everything We Need ———— A Day To Remember
- Loverboy ———— A-Wall
- This One ———— Vance Joy
- Daydream ———— Milk & Bone
- The Love Club ———— Lorde
- Sold out of Love ———— The Nude Party
- Wonderland ———— Taylor Swift
- All Day ———— Jack Botts
- forever & more ———— ROLE MODEL
- Heaven ———— Niall Horan
- the 1 ———— Taylor Swift
- Rollercoaster ———— Bleachers
- Love Story (Taylor's Version) ———— Taylor Swift

Head Over Broken Heels

- We Are Young ———————— fun., Janelle Monáe
- Coastline ———————————— Hollow Coves
- Long Live ——————————— Taylor Swift
- The One ————————————— Kodaline
- Let's Get Married ——————— Bleachers
- Daylight ——————————— Taylor Swift
- I'm with You ———————— Vance Joy
- be my forever —— Christina Perri, Ed Sheerran
- My Everyday ——————————— Volunteer
- Ours ———————————— Taylor Swift
- Where It All Begins ———— Summer Kennedy
- long story short ———————— Taylor Swift

Haley's first book,

ONE LAST HURRAH,

is available now on Amazon!
Signed copies are also on Etsy, PetalsAndPagesByHBD

YOU CAN ALSO FIND ME...

Instagram: @haleyb.designs

TikTok: @haleybrownauthor & @haleyb.designs

Etsy: PetalsAndPagesByHBD

ABOUT THE AUTHOR

Photo by @framesbydestiny

Haley Brown (18), was born and raised on the Gulf Coast. When she's not writing books she's coaching gymnastics, running her own small business, participating in craft shows, going to as many concerts as possible, and traveling. She spends her free time rewatching comfort movies, working on new projects, reading, watching sunsets and sunrises, brainstorming, curating the perfect playlist, and drawing—such as the cover and other small designs found throughout this book!

She self-published her first book, *One Last Hurrah*, in 2022. *Head Over Broken Heels* is her second novel.

Made in United States
North Haven, CT
04 December 2023

45084620R00186